Turning, Charlie froze at the sight of a stunning cinnamon-brown sister navigating her way through a throng of dancing people.

Her long brown hair fell in loose curls across her shoulders while her deep sable eyes twinkled with excitement and two raisin-sized dimples grooved into her apple cheeks. Entranced by her angelic face, it took Charlie longer than normal to take notice of her statuesque curves.

He smacked his lips, but it had nothing to do with the lingering taste of chocolate in his mouth and everything to do with a sudden longing to taste her strawberry-colored lips. Absently, Charlie pulled at his collar and wondered who in the hell had turned up the heat.

Books by Adrianne Byrd

Sinful Chocolate

ADRIANNE BYRD

KIMANI™
ROMANCE

This book, as always, is dedicated to my loyal
Byrdwatchers Group. I couldn't have asked
for a better group of women to cheer me on.

Best of love,
Adrianne

 KIMANI PRESS™

ISBN-13: 978-0-373-86097-5
ISBN-10:   0-373-86097-8

SINFUL CHOCOLATE

Copyright © 2009 by Adrianne Byrd

www.kimanipress.com

Printed in U.S.A.

Dear Reader,

I hope that you enjoy *Sinful Chocolate*. Charlie and Gisella were fun characters to create. This is the second book in the ALPHA PSI ALPHA series. I hope you checked out the first book, *Two Grooms and a Wedding*. The fun never stops with these fine brothers.

Charlie Masters was actually the first character to come to me a few years ago, but I couldn't quite figure out how not to make this story about two people instead of about him and the legions of broken hearts he'd left in his wake. Hopefully I've succeeded.

Gisella is definitely my fantasy self. I'd love to create sinfully delicious chocolate treats and drive men wild with an exotic accent. Maybe next lifetime. Meanwhile, I hope you enjoy *Sinful Chocolate* and then visit my Web site at www.adriannebyrd.com to drop me a line.

Adrianne Byrd

ADRIANNE BYRD

is a national bestselling author who has always preferred to live within the realms of her imagination, where all the men are gorgeous and the women are worth whatever trouble they manage to get into. As an army brat, she traveled throughout Europe and learned to appreciate and value different cultures. Now she calls Georgia home. Looking back, Adrianne believes her passion for writing began at the ripe old age of thirteen. It was also the age that she was introduced to romance novels by a most unlikely source: her fifteen-year-old brother. The book was probably given to her to keep her out of her brother's hair, but it was a gift that changed her life. In books, Adrianne found a way out of her awkward teenage years and into a world of fictional friends that would stay with her for a lifetime. It wasn't long before her imagination took flight and she was writing her own love stories. Within a year, she completed her first book, which she vowed would never see the light of day. Writing remained a hobby until 1994, when a co-worker approached her with an article on Romance Writers of America. Who knew there was an organization of women just like her? By 1996 she had sold her first novel, *Defenseless*, to Kensington Publishing. Her first release received rave reviews from *Romantic Times BOOKreviews* and fans. Her other novels were consistently selected as the magazine's top picks. In 2001, *Say You Love Me,* was nominated for Best Romance at Romance Slam Jam. Her 2003 release *Comfort of a Man* won the *Romantic Times BOOKreviews* Best Multicultural Romance Award; Romance in Color's Readers' Choice awards for Favorite Book, Favorite Hero and Favorite Heroine; a Shades of Romance award; Slam Jam's Emma Award for Favorite Traditional Romance; and Romance in Color's Reviewers' Choice Award for Author of the Year, Book of the Year and Best BET/Arabesque Book. Lastly, *Comfort of a Man* was a 2003 Georgia Romance Writers Maggie finalist for best Contemporary. In 2004, Adrianne released her first romantic-suspense novel, *If You Dare,* with HarperCollins. In 2006, her novel *Measure of a Man* was nominated for Best Multicultural Romance while her Harper Torch novel *Deadly Double* was nominated for an Emma Award. In 2007, she won an eHarlequin.com Joey Award.

Chapter 1

"Surprise!"

Charlie Masters clutched a hand over his heart and jumped back from his front door. Before his mind could register what was happening, the large crowd of people crammed into his Buckhead high-rise broke out in song.

"Happy birthday to you! Happy birthday to you!"

At last a smile broke wide across his full lips as he finally crossed the threshold into his apartment where black-and-gold balloons showered down on his head. "You guys shouldn't have," he said in the middle of their song.

His smiling and jubilant friends parted like the Red Sea to allow a magnificent four-tier, circular chocolate cake to be rolled out to the center of the living room.

Charlie moved forward, taken aback by the decorative

dessert. Each layer showcased multiple ribbons of dark and white chocolate. On top, the ribbons looked more like a gigantic Christmas bow with the number thirty-four sparkling in the center.

Impressed and touched by the gesture, Charlie blushed like a prepubescent teenager until his friends finally ended their song and erupted into a thunderous applause.

"Thank you, guys. Thanks. You're the best."

"Are you just going to stare at it all night, or are you going to make a wish and blow out the candles?"

Charlie turned to his right and beamed a smile toward his best friend and fraternity brother Derrick Knight and his wife Isabella. "Hold your horses, man. Can't a brother just enjoy the moment?"

The guests laughed heartily.

Derrick rolled his eyes, but his smile remained as wide as Charlie's.

To his left, his other three Kappa Psi Kappa brothers cut in, "C'mon man. Make a wish."

"Yeah. You're holding up the music," Taariq added.

Make a wish. Wouldn't it be great if he could fix his mounting problems by simply making a wish? Feeling the weight of everyone's stare, Charlie played the good sport by closing his eyes, leaning forward and finally blowing out the candles.

Another round of thunderous applause ensued and a second later, Rick Ross poured out of his surround-sound speakers, and most of the crowd paired off to get their grooves on. The rest of them crowded around Charlie and pounded his back in congratulations. It felt like most of the guys were trying to break his spine in half.

Before Charlie could ask his Kappa brothers how they'd managed to plan this whole thing without him catching wind of it, Hylan moved up behind him and jammed him into a headlock and razed the top of his head with his knuckles.

"Hey, old man. What did ya wish for?"

Charlie chuckled despite his inability to breathe.

"He can't tell you that," Isabella said, coming to his defense. "If he tells, then it won't come true."

Hylan grunted, but released Charlie before he passed out.

In retaliation, Charlie popped Hylan on the back of the head, and then the two raised their dukes as if they were really considering squaring off for a fight.

Taariq rolled his eyes and sucked his teeth. "You two cut it out."

Still smiling, Hylan and Charlie dropped their fists and instead gave each other a shoulder bump.

"Happy birthday, man," Hylan said. "You're…" Their conversation trailed off when a Halle Berry look-alike strolled past laughing and shaking her romp to the hard bass pounding all around them. "Excuse me, fellahs," Hylan said, adjusting an invisible tie. "But booty calls."

Charlie and the gang laughed as Hylan strolled off in a George Jefferson-imitation strut.

"A steak dinner says he'll strike out," Charlie said, sliding a hand into his pocket and rocking back on his heels.

Taariq frowned. "You know her?"

Charlie nodded. "Yvette. I tried to hook up with her a

couple of years ago, but her *girlfriend,* if you know what I mean, nearly took me out."

The fraternity brothers chuckled then swung their heads back in Hylan's direction to watch in giddy anticipation of his crash and burn.

Yvette beamed a beautiful smile at Hylan and even fluttered a hand across her heart.

Taariq leaned toward Charlie when Hylan's mack game seemed to be working. "Maybe she's swung back to our side of the fence," he whispered.

"Oh ye of little faith." Charlie smirked. "Three, two, one."

Right on time, a three-foot-eleven woman rushed onto the scene and managed to work her way in between Hylan and Yvette.

Isabella gasped. *"That's* her girlfriend?"

Hylan stared down at the small woman in open confusion…right up until the time the woman dealt a deadly left hook into the family jewels.

"Ooooh." Charlie and the Kappa boys cringed and covered their own packages in union as they watched their brother double over in pain.

The angry little woman snatched her girlfriend's hand, and together they marched off into the dancing crowd.

Isabella couldn't help but join in. "I don't think I've ever seen anything like that in my entire life."

"Been there, done that." Charlie shook his head. "I wore a cup to the clubs for a full year after Mighty Mouse dealt me the same blow."

Taariq, Derrick and Isabella laughed.

A crouched Hylan returned to their intimate circle in defeat.

"So how did it go?" Derrick baited, wrapping an arm around his wife. "Get the digits?"

"I don't think she's my type," Hylan croaked. "Damn. Is it just me, or is the room spinning?"

"It's just you," the gang responded and then burst out laughing again.

Still chuckling, Charlie gave a quick scan of the room to survey the selection of beauties his buddies had rounded up for the evening. If anyone knew his type it would be his Kappa brothers.

After a week of battling to keep his company, Masters Holdings, from plunging into bankruptcy, Charlie needed a distraction. Burying himself into something along the lines of five-foot-nine with a lot of curves was right up his alley. The thicker the better.

Judging by the number of female gazes that drifted his way, Charlie was going to have a good night. A very good night.

Taariq threw the best damn parties in Atlanta, and it was clear he'd spared no expense for Charlie's thirty-fourth birthday bash. Actually, calling them merely women was a serious disservice. They were more like works of art.

"I know that look." Taariq laughed, swinging another hard pound against Charlie's back. "I guess that means we can give you our gifts early."

Frowning, Charlie faced the group again. In sync, they each rolled out a sleeve of gold-packaged condoms.

Isabella couldn't stop herself from giggling.

"Try not to use them all in one night," Derrick chuckled.

"Funny." Charlie rolled his eyes when the gang draped the condoms around his neck like Mardi Gras beads.

"You know I've been waiting hours so I can have a slice of this cake," Isabella said, drawing his attention from his search of women in the room.

Charlie took another look at the elaborate cake, once again impressed with the intricate details. "Chocolate. My favorite." He picked up the knife but hesitated slicing the beautiful dessert.

"Derrick told me you loved chocolate. So I got you something a little different: molten chocolate cake. The center is filled with raspberry jelly." Isabella beamed and clutched her hands together. "I found this wonderful new shop downtown. The owner is a master." She glanced around. "Where is she?" Isabella grabbed his hand. "I can't wait for you to meet her."

Charlie selected a corner and gently cut a slice. "Here you go," he said, grabbing a paper plate and serving her. After handing it over, he noticed a smudge of frosting on his finger and licked it off.

"Hmm." His eyes bulged in shock at the sinfully delicious chocolate as it melted in his mouth.

Isabella lit up. "Wonderful, isn't it?" She grabbed a fork and then held out a piece of the cake for him to taste. "Here, try it."

"Heeey!" Derrick stepped forward and draped a possessive arm around his wife's waist. "I'm the only man you're supposed to be feeding cake to." He even managed to look wounded.

Charlie ignored Derrick's fake jealousy act and took a bite of the cake Isabella offered. "Hmm. Damn!" Hands down, it was the best cake he'd ever tasted. He better not tell his mother that.

Isabella's excitement grew. "Fantastic, isn't it? I swear this woman is going to be the next big thing," Isabella gushed and then turned toward her husband. "I'm telling you we need to invest in her shop."

Derrick sighed dramatically, but he wasn't fooling anyone. Where Isabella was concerned, Charlie's best friend would deny her nothing. After a year of marriage, the couple still behaved as though they were coasting on an extended honeymoon—probably to the dismay of Isabella's father, who had his mind and heart set on his only daughter marrying a prominent political ally and another Kappa Psi Kappa brother named Randall Jarrett.

No one ever mentioned how Isabella was once, technically, engaged to two men at the same time, or how her father had arranged to have Derrick held hostage while trying to force her to marry someone she didn't love. But they *did* talk and laugh every chance they could about Derrick, Randall *and* Reverend Williams falling headfirst into a Lady Justice water fountain and duking it out in front of Washington's political elite moments before Isabella was to walk down the aisle.

"Where's Stanley?" Charlie asked.

The group looked around.

"He's gotta be around here somewhere," Taariq said, frowning. "He better not bother the DJ. I keep telling that boy that white men can't rap and I better not catch him on the mic. I have a rep, you know."

"What about Eminem?" Charlie asked.

"I reserve judgment until I see the man's daddy. You know what I mean?"

"Yeah, whatever."

"All right, all right." Charlie popped his collar. "I know you have some Cristal floating around here."

Taariq reached out and grabbed two flutes from a passing server. "Yo, here you go, bro." He handed a glass to Charlie. "Cheers!"

"Check it. One, two. One, two," Stanley rapped into the microphone. "I'm a white boy and a frat boy—"

"All, hell naw," Taariq cursed. "They gave Stanley the mic. "Charlie—"

"Yeah, I'm cool. Handle your business." Charlie chuckled and waved him off.

People in the crowd started booing.

Charlie sliced himself a piece of cake. As he chewed he couldn't stop moaning. He tried to stop, but damn. *What exactly is in this stuff?*

"Oh, there she is," Isabella said, glancing over Charlie's shoulder and waving.

Turning, Charlie froze as a stunning cinnamon-brown sister navigated her way through a throng of dancing people. Her long brown hair fell in loose curls across her shoulders while her deep sable eyes twinkled with excitement and two raisin-sized dimples grooved into her apple cheeks. Entranced by the angelic vision, it took Charlie longer than normal to take notice of her statuesque curves.

He smacked his lips, but it had nothing to with the lingering taste of chocolate in his mouth and everything to do with a sudden longing to taste her strawberry-colored lips. Absently, Charlie pulled at his collar and wondered who in the hell turned up the heat.

In Charlie's mind, the woman was moving in slow motion—like a classier version of Bo Derek in the movie *10*. The beauty's breasts had a slight jiggle as she walked and her hips swayed in a strange, but hypnotic, rhythm.

"Happy birthday to me," Charlie mumbled under his breath while his erection pressed hard against the inseam of his pants.

Isabella looped an arm around the mysterious woman's waist and then led her to their small circle. "Gisella, I'd like for you meet the man of the hour, Charles Masters—but everyone calls him Charlie. Charlie, this is Gisella Jacobs, the owner of Sinful Chocolate. She made your cake."

"A pleasure to meet you," Charlie said, offering to take her hand. "The cake is delicious."

"Likewise." Gisella's accented voice was musical yet husky, a heady combination. "You have a lot of friends," she added, glancing around. "I hope you don't mind my crashing and networking for new business. Isabella assured me that you wouldn't mind."

Charlie cocked his head while the corners of his lips curled with open pleasure. "You're French," he announced, moving closer. "How erotic."

Gisella's arched brows rose in amusement. "Erotic?"

Even the way she said the word sent pleasure rippling down his spine and added a sweet ache to his throbbing hard-on. "Come on now," Charlie said, erasing the last remaining inches between them. "Surely I'm not the only red-blooded American man who's been enslaved by your…" His eyes roamed yet again. "Accent."

"Oh, he *is* good," Isabella whispered, turning toward her husband.

Charlie had forgotten about their audience.

Derrick nodded and proceeded to pull his wife away. "Let me get you out of here before you fall under his spell and I have to fight for you all over again."

Taariq and Hylan also didn't linger for a brick wall to fall on their heads. They quickly turned their attention to a couple of other women floating by.

Gisella looked stunned at how fast everyone disappeared and left her alone with a man with predatory eyes and a wolfish smile. Maybe she should grab one of the white napkins from the table and wave it as a flag of surrender.

"I'm glad Isabella told you to come. I like making new friends." Charlie couldn't stop his gaze from roaming again. By his shrewd calculations, her measurements were a perfect 36-24-36. Lord, this was shaping up to be one hell of a birthday.

"Interesting party favors."

"Huh?" Charlie followed her line of vision to the condoms draped around his neck. "Oh. Well. You want one?"

Gisella blinked and took a step back.

"Okay. *That* didn't come out right." He laughed.

Gisella took another precautionary step back. The man looked as if he was going to devour her right there in front of everyone. "Well, like I said. I'm just trying to drum up new business," she said, trying to swallow her nervous tremor.

"You're not going to have a problem with that once everyone tastes this wonderful creation. How long have you been baking?"

Her smile brightened again. "All my life. My *mère* and *grandmère* still run a shop in Paris."

Gisella's accent enraptured Charlie.

A woman to their right emitted a low moan of orgasmic pleasure. "Oh, my God, this cake is off the chain." The woman turned to her companion. "Here, taste this."

Gisella's cheeks blushed a rich sienna. "I love baking and cooking. Food is life, no?"

Charlie just smiled. "Have you ever heard that the quickest way to a man's heart is through his stomach?"

Eyes twinkling, Gisella's lips turned up into a sly smile. "If I wanted your heart, I would just take it."

Charlie cocked his head with a bemused grin, but when he opened his mouth for a quick retort, a pair of hands slipped over his eyes.

"Guess who." A high-pitched feminine voice floated over the shell of Charlie's ear while a small set of breasts pressed into his back.

Not now. He controlled his irritation while he forced a smile. "Let me see now," he said, wondering how to get out of a potentially sticky situation. "Could this possibly be my favorite woman in the whole wide world?"

"And who would that be?" the woman asked with attitude edging her voice.

Charlie reached to uncover his eyes. "Dear ole Mom, of course," he answered, pulling away the small hands and turning around with his ready-made smile still hugging his lips.

"Hey, you." He still didn't know the name of the smiling beauty, with a short spiked haircut and eyes the color of maple, but he was determined not to go down in flames. "You came!"

The woman's face lit up with pleasure. "I wouldn't have missed your birthday for the world." She inched closer and lowered her voice in a conspiratorial whisper. "Especially after that wonderful weekend last month."

Charlie was still clueless to the woman's identity. After all, that was four weekends ago, and he was never without company on any of them.

"Well, I'm glad you made it," he whispered. His mind scrambled for a way to get rid of her so that he could get back to Gisella.

"I hope you're saving one of those for me," she cooed, pulling one sleeve of condoms from around his neck. "In fact—" she leaned in close "—why don't we slip away upstairs and I give you your birthday gift?" She grinded her hips against his to ensure he caught her meaning.

Charlie's brows jumped at the suggestion. "Why don't you meet me up there in about twenty minutes? I gotta say hi to a few more people first."

The beauty sucked in her bottom lip and gave him a wink. "Don't leave me waiting too long." Still holding the sleeve of condoms, she turned and switched her hips as she moved through the crowd.

Charlie sighed and then turned back to address Gisella. She was gone.

Glancing around the perimeter of the room, Charlie's heart pounded in double-time. He moved through the crowd, searching.

"How about a dance?" a new woman asked, looping her arms around Charlie's neck.

"Not right now." He tried to pry the woman's arms away but she locked her hands together and kept him ensnared between her arms. "I'm looking for someone," he confessed.

"Another woman?" she asked, inching up an eyebrow.

Charlie glanced down and recognized Lexi—another fling from last month. "Oh, hey." He changed up his program. "How are you? I've been meaning to call."

"I just bet you have," she said, smiling though her tone held a lethal edge. "I should have listened to my girlfriends and stayed away from you."

Charlie's lips curled wickedly. "Then why didn't you?"

Lexi hesitated and then allowed her eyes to roam down the front of his body. "Because I wanted to see whether you'd live up to your reputation."

He arched an eyebrow, his ego expanding. "How did I do?"

She flashed him an incredibly white smile. "You're a cocky sonofabitch."

"*That* is what makes me so adorable."

"One of these days…"

From the corner of Charlie's eyes he caught sight of Gisella heading toward the door. He finally pulled Lexi's hands from around his neck and winked at her. "Hold on a second."

"Yeah. Right. I won't hold my breath."

Charlie plowed back into the crowd and tried to

maneuver his way to the door. But every few steps another woman would grab him by the arm, the neck and even his crotch to ask why he hadn't called them in such a long time.

At the door, Gisella stopped and kissed Isabella on each cheek and then waved goodbye to her.

"No. Wait," he called after her, but the loud music swallowed his voice and a throng of women kept pulling at him. By the time he made it to the door and then glanced down the hallway of his Buckhead high-rise, Gisella was long gone.

Chapter 2

"He's not my type," Gisella repeated to herself. No matter how many times she made the declaration, a part of her rebelled at the notion. The thought just kept coming to the forefront of her mind how handsome-no-how *fine* Charlie Masters was. From the moment that six-two, golden brown Adonis strolled inside his high-rise apartment, Gisella could hardly take her eyes off of him.

The man exuded confidence and possessed an undeniable sexual prowess that dampened his fair share of panty liners whenever he walked by. And those eyes—playful hazel green—that sparkled if you were fortunate enough to hold his attention.

No wonder every woman in the room was practically drooling and shamelessly throwing themselves at him. It wasn't surprising that he looked as if he was reveling in his element.

From the moment she'd slipped her hand into his, there was a powerful magnetic pull toward him, which was right on course since she had an affinity for bad boys, the very habit that she'd promised herself to break.

With a determined shake of her head, Gisella erased Charlie's image just as she arrived at her car in the high-rise parking garage. "Forget about him," she mumbled under her breath as she unlocked the car and slid in behind the wheel.

But that was easier said than done. After moving over four thousand miles to get away from the last playa extraordinaire who'd broken her heart, Robert Beauvais, she swore her next man would be the more stable kind—the marrying kind. When his name and image floated across her head, she couldn't help but roll her eyes. Of all the men she could have fallen for, she had to fall in love with an international male model.

If there was one life lesson learned, it was to never trust a man who's prettier than you are.

Gisella laughed at herself as she pulled out onto the highway and headed toward her half sister's apartment in downtown Atlanta. The distance wasn't too far, but with so many one-way roads, it was easy for her to keep getting turned around.

By the time she made it to Anna's place, it was beyond late, and her sister had already gone to bed for the night. It was just as well because the last thing she wanted to do was play Twenty Questions.

Since Gisella's move to America, Anna had taken her

role as protector a bit too seriously. Gisella suspected it had a lot to do with Anna's obsession with police shows and forensic files. For her, trouble lurked around every corner, especially if there was a man involved. Where Gisella had one ugly breakup, Anna had a string of them.

Despite being beautiful, men had lied to, stolen from, beaten up and slept around on Anna. You name it, she had been through it, and when Gisella called her crying about Robert's infidelity, Anna convinced her to leave France and start over with a new life in Atlanta.

Nine months later, Gisella wasn't exactly sorry she'd made the move, but she realized that she had underestimated just how broken and bitter her sister really was. Once a month, Anna and a handful of her college girlfriends would host the Lonely Hearts Club. It was supposed to be a book club, but its real function was for the women to get together and gripe about men.

At first Gisella welcomed the sisterhood meetings as a place to vent over the demise of her engagement, but at what point were these women going to move on?

Gisella used the meetings as the first step in healing.

Anna used the group as a monthly soapbox.

After tiptoeing to her sister's room, Gisella slowly turned the knob and opened the door, then eased her head inside. Under the soft glow of light from the nightstand table, Gisella found Anna's sleeping form curled up on her side with a thick book next to her. Smiling, Gisella eased into the room and made it over to the bed to gently remove her sister's reading glasses from her face.

Anna moaned and stirred, but she didn't wake. "Good

night, big sis," Gisella whispered, leaning down and placing a kiss against her sister's forehead before turning off the light.

Gisella crept to her bedroom and quickly kicked off her heels and slid out of her clothes before heading toward the adjoining bathroom. In the short time it took for her to make it to the shower, Charlie Masters had eased into her thoughts, and a smile had curved its way back onto her lips.

Humph. Humph. Humph. It really should be a crime for a man to be that hot, that fine, that *sexy*.

Without meaning to, Gisella made a few calculations and realized it had been more than a year since she had last experienced the touch of a man. Never mind the whole seduction of kissing and…well, just getting laid.

Sighing as she stood underneath the spray of hot water, Gisella allowed her active imagination to take flight. Still smiling, she pretended Charlie had joined her in the bathroom's billowing steam and that it was his hands instead of the mesh sponge massaging liquid soap across her soft skin.

Gisella moaned and lolled her head back as if giving her imaginary lover full access to her slender neck.

"You taste like strawberries and chocolate," murmured Fantasy Charlie, nibbling on her ear. His slick hands now roaming around her body and then cupped her full breasts. Instantly, her dusky brown nipples puckered and then throbbed for attention.

Charlie's rich laughter bounced off the bathroom tiles before his head dipped low and took a hardened nipple into his mouth. Despite knowing this whole thing was just a fantasy, Gisella's knees still went weak as the shower's hot droplets substituted for Charlie's mouth and talented tongue.

"Does that feel good, baby?"

She barely managed to croak out a "Yes" while an army of strawberry bubbles roamed and marched toward the springy black vee of curls between her legs. Charlie's fingers followed the sudsy front line and then penetrated her with smooth gentle strokes.

Gisella hiked up one leg onto tub's ledge and gave her fantasy lover better access to her pulsing cherry. There was also no mistaking the change in her breathing. Soon her temperature rose and it had nothing to with the hot cascading water.

Long strokes.

Short strokes.

Gisella's moans climbed higher and higher. In her ear, Fantasy Charlie kept urging her to, *"Come for me, baby. That's it."*

"Ooooh, yes," she sighed, her body tingling.

"That's a good girl."

Toes curling, Gisella's sighs and moans continued while she imagined the feel of Charlie's rock-hard erection pressed against her round bottom.

"You comin' for me?"

"Y-yessss."

"What's my name, baby?" he asked, his fingers now plunging deep into her core.

"Ch-Charlie." The moment his name crested her lips, her inner muscles tightened while she buckled against his hand. When her orgasm hit, her imaginary world exploded behind her closed eyelids, and her face was momentarily submerged under the shower's steady stream.

It was at that moment the heat disappeared, Fantasy Charlie vanished along with the shower's rolling steam, and the water turned into stabbing icicles. She jumped back and nearly tripped over the shower mat. Equilibrium restored, Gisella laughed at herself as she rushed to shut off the water.

Once out of the tub, she wrapped a plush towel around her body and made a second one into a turban over her wet hair. Walking back into her bedroom, her teeth chattered, and her skin pimpled with fresh goose bumps when the cool breeze from the air conditioner kissed her skin.

One thing was for sure: Gisella was a hell of a lot more relaxed after her session with Fantasy Charlie.

She giggled and then fell into a heap across the bed. The clock on the nightstand read one o'clock a.m. Gisella sighed contentedly and promised to get up in a moment to slip into her nightclothes and dry her hair, but before she knew it, she unfurled a few wide yawns and curled against her pillow.

Immediately, Charlie Masters resurfaced in her mind. "I'm not supposed to think about him," she mumbled. A man like Charlie was dangerous.

Plus, how desperate must she be to fantasize about a man she'd just met and had talked to for less than five minutes?

But what a man.

Burrowing herself into the bedsheets and comforter, the devil on her left shoulder argued with the angel on her right. In the end, Gisella saw nothing wrong with carrying on with her fantasy lover. As long as she never *acted* on her impulse or actually tried to hook up with the handsome playboy, what harm could it do?

"No harm at all," Fantasy Charlie whispered as he brushed a kiss against her satiny shoulder.

Gisella rolled onto her back and stared up into his hypnotic hazel green eyes.

"I have a question," he said, reaching beneath her pillow and then withdrawing her hidden vibrator. *"Mind if we play with this?"*

Chapter 3

Charlie woke up early Sunday morning the same way he woke up every Sunday morning: completely satisfied and with a curvaceous beauty at his side. What was the girl's name again—Marcia, Jan or Cindy? Maybe he was thinking of *The Brady Bunch*. Blair, Jo, Tootie—no, that was the *Facts of Life*.

The woman moaned softly as she turned and wiggled her rump against his hip—a silent invitation and a coy way of letting him know that she was no longer asleep. Hard and ready, he was more than willing to RSVP her invite when the phone rang.

Mentally, he wrestled with whether he should answer, but then relented when his gaze read the digital clock. Groaning, he snatched up the phone. "I'm up, Taariq."

"Yeah? Well, you're late," he said, irritation dripping through the phone line. "It's bad enough you dissed us at the party last night for that Beyoncé wannabe. By the way, how was she?"

Charlie glanced out of the corner of his eyes to skim over the woman's voluptuous form imprinted beneath the silk sheets. "A gentleman never tells."

"Has anyone ever told you you're one lucky S.O.B? You eased up on her two seconds before I did."

"You snooze, you lose." He smiled and sat up. "Give me about an hour, and I'll be right over."

"One hour." Taariq huffed. "I'm going to hold you to it."

"Whatever." Charlie hung up and turned his attention back to—Penny? No, that was *Good Times*. Well, when in doubt, he relied on his favorite pet name. "Hey, baby girl." He eased a hand beneath the sheet and caressed her soft skin. "I really hate to have to do this, but I, um, I'm afraid it's time to get up."

She emitted another soft moan, but then gracefully rolled over to her side to face him. Big, beautiful cat-shaped eyes fluttered open to reveal an intriguing shade of gray.

"Do we really have to get up?" she inquired, curling the corners of her full lips.

Charlie stared at the nymph in his bed as though it was the first time he'd seen her. Her face was devoid of makeup except the slightest hint of red lipstick. She was stunning. "Denise," he murmured.

"You remembered. I'm impressed."

"How could I ever forget? Denise just like in *The Cosby Show*," Charlie covered smoothly.

"Do you always try to do name associations with TV shows?"

Charlie blinked. "Not always."

"Then I guess the rumors are false."

"Rumors?"

Denise's tinted lips widened across her face. "C'mon. You have to know you're a man with quite a reputation." Her eyes traveled down his chest and settled on his erection. "Not all of it bad."

Charlie's ego inflated. "Glad to hear it."

Something stirred at the foot of the bed and since Charlie didn't have any animals, he jumped, but then quickly relaxed when the covers lifted and Samantha's—like in *Sex and the City*—tussled head peeked out. "Are you sure it's time to get out of bed?"

Charlie's smile slid wider. "Did you two have something else in mind?"

"As a matter of fact—" the beauty tossed the sheet back from her body to give him a clear view of what she was offering "—I have a *few* things in mind."

His erection throbbed and robbed him of sufficient oxygen for him to think clearly. At last a smile rolled across his lips. "To hell with Taariq."

"*You* let her meet Charlie Masters?" Nicole, Anna's busybody best friend roared incredulously. She pretended to rub wax out of her ears. "Please tell me I'm hearing things."

A bored and sleep-intoxicated Anna struggled to rake her fingers through her frizzy hair before turning her attention to her large mug of coffee. "Gisella is a grown woman and more than capable of keeping her legs closed."

Nicole's eyes narrowed. "No woman can think straight when Charlie is on the prowl. How many times have I told you girls that?" She glanced around the four-member Lonely Hearts Club.

"At least a million," Anna droned.

"Exactly." Nicole crossed her arms and glared at her best friend. "I knew this was going to happen. I swear Charlie has like this radar whenever a beautiful new woman moves into this city. Hell, I'm surprised it took him nine months to find her."

The other women snickered at the joke, which only encouraged Nicole to stay perched atop her soapbox. "Wake up, Anna, your sister is exactly Charlie's type, and he'll be all over her like white on rice."

Jade, one of the founding members of the group frowned. "What's Charlie's type?"

"Anything with breasts and a pulse," Nicole shot back.

"Damn. I better hide Sasha, too." Anna bent down and picked up her orange-and-yellow tabby cat that kept mewing at her ankles.

"She's telling the truth," said Emmadonna, a plus-size beauty with a mountainous chip on her shoulder, nodding in agreement. "I met the famous dog at a club a couple of years back, thinking I was safe since he spent half the night dancing with the same old anorexic-looking chicks until he brushed up on me."

"Ooh?" the other women chorused.

"Next thing I know, he was all up in my ear, saying only a dog wants to play with some bones."

The women laughed.

"Girl, I played it cool for about two minutes before I jumped him and showed him how us big girls worked it out. Nahwhatimean?" She held up her hands and received a train of high fives while the room filled with new squeals of laughter.

"If you didn't see the devil horns and tail then you weren't looking hard enough," Nicole said, rolling her eyes.

"Oh, I was looking, all right," Emmadonna said. "All I saw was a tall brother with money, class, sophistication… and if I'm not mistaken, a dash of thug in him. Every girl needs a little thug in their lives."

"That man has a trail of broken hearts that stretches halfway around the globe." Nicole's hands settled on her thick hips. "Charlie's a diehard playa, and any woman who thinks she can change him, which is every woman he's ever come in contact with, is just kidding herself."

"Including you," Jade said, easing back into the leather couch with a knowing smile.

"Yes, including me." Nicole squared her shoulders. "Of course, *I* never became a notch on his bedpost. I had a little more sense than that."

Anna rolled her eyes and yawned. "Anyone want some more coffee?" She shuffled toward the kitchen. "If I have to wake up, I might as well do it the right way."

"I could've slept with him if I wanted," Nicole said to Anna's back.

"I hope you like Folgers."

"Ignore if you want, but back in college I was considered a fine catch myself," Nicole reminded her.

"Of course, I think we might have some Taster's Choice in here," Anna kept on, unfazed.

Nicole rolled her eyes. "Folgers is fine."

Anna rustled through the cabinets for a few minutes and then fumbled with the coffeemaker. All this talk about Charlie was hitting a little too close for home. She had her own history with the infamous playa and she'd rather just forget the whole incident. She certainly didn't want to talk about it.

Nicole glanced down at her watch. "It's noon. I bet you anything, Charlie is lying next to some chick right now trying to figure out the best way to get her out of there."

"Okay, now you're creepin' me out." Anna hit the Brew button. "You know just a little too much about the man's modus operandi."

"All playas have the same M.O. Hit and run."

"I still say Gisella is smarter than that. She was just hired to make the man's cake. She's hardly looking to leap back into another relationship after what her ex just put her through."

"Charlie doesn't *do* relationships."

"And Gisella doesn't believe in one-night stands."

Emmadonna, with supersonic ears for all things gossip, cackled from the living room. "Girl, please. Every woman has had at least one."

Anna and Nicole rejoined the women in the living room.

"I say," Nicole continued, "the only way a woman can avoid getting caught up in Charlie Masters's dog trap is to run the other way when you see him strolling down the sidewalk."

"Amen" circled around the room along with another series of high fives before the women burst out laughing.

Curious about the commotion in the apartment, Gisella finished dressing and joined her sister's friends in the living room. "What's so funny?"

The minute she walked into the room, all the laughter was suddenly sucked out of the air and everyone began straightening and fidgeting in their seats.

Gisella cast her gaze around the room as suspicion crept up her spine. "*Parlez-vous de moi?*"

Anna shooed Sasha off her lap and stood up. "Don't be silly, Gisella," she said, shuffling over and draping her arm around her shoulders. "We weren't talking about you—exactly."

"No, we were talking about your birthday boy last night," Nicole said, piping up.

Gisella's face flushed. Had her sister heard her in her room last night? Oh, Lord, hadn't she called out his name a few times?

Nicole pointed. "Look at her face. Something *did* happen last night."

Anna's arm fell from Gisella's shoulders. "You didn't!"

"Didn't what?" Gisella asked, thoroughly confused.

"Sleep with the enemy," Anna said. "Charlie Masters is the biggest man-whore in Atlanta."

"And that's putting it nicely," Nicole agreed.

Gisella groaned before she could stop herself. Didn't these girls ever give it a rest? Men were not the enemy. "Relax," she huffed. "Nothing happened. I went to network, remember?"

Unconvinced, Nicole planted her hands on her hips. "Did you meet the birthday boy?"

Four sets of eyes locked onto Gisella and waited.

"I met him." Gisella shrugged. "He said he loved the cake, and then I took off."

Anna smiled as her arm magically reappeared around her shoulder. "See? I told you she knew how to handle herself."

Ivy, the petite and soft-spoken member of their group, voiced her suspicions. "You mean Charlie didn't even try to hit on you?"

Gisella shook her head, even though the memory of their light flirting replayed in her head. "Nope."

"Damn." Emmadonna chuckled and eased back into her seat. "We really are living in the last days."

Chapter 4

Life had gone from bad to worse.

It was the only way Charlie could explain it. His company, Masters Holdings, continued to edge toward bankruptcy. Hopefully, his upcoming trip to South Africa would change all of that. His bid for a lucrative government contract was all that stood between him and financial ruin. The housing market combined with the credit crisis had formed the perfect storm to sink his financial ship. He was going to lose everything. The high-rise. The cars. The boat. The plane. His lifestyle.

To make matters worse, Charlie had been less than forthcoming with his frat brothers. How could he be, when they were still very rich and very successful in their own right? The last thing he wanted was to be labeled the failure of the group, nor did he want anyone's sympathy.

After all, he did have his pride.

No. Charlie shook his head. He was going to rebound from this. He had to.

First, he had to survive this basketball game. Hylan and Taariq were running rings around him today, and Derrick looked ready to kick him to the curb and pick Stanley as his partner.

But something was changing. Charlie felt it the moment Hylan passed Taariq the basketball and he launched into trying to block the next shot. Sure, he was in shape. He worked out five days a week at his local gym. Pumped iron, practiced kickboxing and swam like a fish in their indoor pool. And every Sunday afternoon, like today, he and his frat brothers got together on the half-court at Derrick's spacious estate in Stone Mountain for a few friendly games.

Bottom line: he was in shape.

So what was this change he was feeling in his body? The same change he'd been feeling since the moment he blew out the candles on his birthday cake.

I'm getting old.

Charlie frowned at the continuous thought circling his mind. Trying to dispel the notion, he pushed himself a little harder, ignored a few straining muscles and wiped the pouring sweat off his forehead with the back of his arms like windshield wipers in the midst of a thunderstorm.

Still, he didn't feel as aerodynamic as he had in college. Why weren't his other frat brothers struggling?

Taariq faked a shot, Charlie jumped and a collection of

muscles in his lower back throbbed in protest. Recovering, he jerked to his left, intersected Taariq's running dribble for a clean steal.

"Yeah!" Derrick shouted as he did his best to clear the perimeter for Charlie to take his shot. Some people who'd watched them play in the past thought it was a bit odd for the teams to be divided as three on two. Those same people quickly understood when they saw how Stanley epitomized the term: white men can't jump…or shoot, dribble, block or run.

"Take your shot!" Derrick shouted. "Take your shot."

Charlie took aim and then launched the ball. Everyone stopped to watch its perfect arch. Taariq, Hylan and Stanley groaned when it swished beautifully inside the netting.

The game tied, Charlie and Derrick whooped in excitement and pumped their fists in the air.

Charlie took a moment to bend at the waist and chugged in a few deep gulps of air.

"You okay, hot shot?" Taariq asked, eyeing him up and down.

"Never better." Charlie righted himself and forced a smile.

Taariq shrugged off his concern and turned back to wait for Stanley to toss the ball back into play.

Charlie's resentment toward the other guys' boundless energy returned. Of course, they could be faking, too, he realized. He couldn't see any of them admitting to the pull of aging.

Kicking it into overdrive, Charlie tapped into the energy reserves he had left and started zigzagging in between the fellahs. But somewhere along the line, he lost his mind.

That was the only explanation for his delusion of being like Michael Jordan in 1989 and launching across the court with the song "I Believe I Can Fly" playing in his head.

Flying wasn't the problem.

It was landing.

The ball swooshed through the hoop, giving him and Derrick the winning two points. However, when Charlie's feet hit the concrete, his ankles folded like paper.

"Ooh, damn!" the Kappa brothers chorused and winced at the same time.

"Owww!" The sound that erupted from his throat wasn't unlike a roaring lion. But when Charlie looked down and saw the odd angle of his foot, his deep bass disappeared and he sounded like, what Derrick would later call, a wailing banshee.

"Oh, my God, I've died and gone to heaven," moaned Waqueisha, Isabella's good friend and Delta Phi Theta sorority sister, as she bit into another one of Gisella's chocolate truffles. "I know you said the girl was good, but damn!"

Waqueisha was the epitome of the round the way girl. She wore a lot of hair weave, tight clothes and was still rockin' bamboo earrings. Despite all that she was a very successful entertainment publicist.

"Everything just tastes so fantastic," said Rayne, another soror and a timid elementary schoolteacher. "I want two dozen of these chocolate coconut nuggets. Make that three dozen."

Gisella beamed at the women. "Isabella, I can't thank you enough," she gushed, rushing to fill the ladies' orders.

"It's been crazy since that birthday party, and every day I'm getting calls and orders from people that say you've recommended my shop."

"You can thank me by agreeing to let me be your business partner," Isabella said. She'd given up tax law when she became Mrs. Derrick Knight and searched high and low for a career change. Since she found her courage and stopped being the person her parents wanted her to be, she'd spent the last year doing some much needed soul searching. She wanted to be involved in something that inspired her and elicited her passion.

"I'm flattered," Gisella said, shaking her head. "But going national just seems so grand, *oui?* I just like things simple. I bake and make treats because I like making people happy. I don't like making a big fuss of everything."

"You won't have to," Isabella said. "You bake, and I'll fuss over the big stuff."

"Yeah," Waqueisha said. "No one out-fusses our girl Izzy."

Isabella frowned and Waqueisha shrugged. "What? I was just trying to help you make the sale."

Isabella raced behind the counter and draped an arm around Gisella's shoulder. "Just picture it." She swept one hand up toward the ceiling as she described her vision. "Sinful Chocolate being packaged and sold in shops just like this one all across America, your grandmother's recipes putting smiles on millions of faces," she waxed enthusiastically.

"And depositing an insane amount of money into your bank account," Rayne added.

Gisella smiled and shook her head. "*Je ne pense pas.* Money is not the most important thing in the world."

Waqueisha and Rayne's mouths fell open.

"What?" Gisella asked, frowning at the two women.

"You really aren't from around here, are you?" Waqueisha said.

Gisella finally laughed. "Am I really all that different?" She glanced around. "I've seen you with your husband. Can you really tell me that the things that truly make you happy are attached to how much money he makes or what kind of car he drives?"

Isabella's face flushed a deep burgundy. "No."

"You see?" Gisella gave a smug smile to Waqueisha and Rayne. "Material things are what distract people when they're not following their hearts. Things like family, laughter, food and love are the real keys to happiness."

Waqueisha blinked. "Damn. That sounded like it should be on a Hallmark card."

Charlie and his frat brothers soon discovered that the emergency room was no place for an emergency. Bored and in no hurry, the E.R. nurses were more interested in exchanging gossip than helping the sick and injured. Instead, Charlie was stuck watching a bunch of unruly children run around hyped up on sodas and vending machine snacks while a loop of the same news from T. J. Holmes and the rest of the CNN weekend crew played every fifteen minutes.

Finally, Hylan had to ask. "Man, what the hell were you thinking?"

Derrick, Taariq and Stanley all covered their mouths and snickered.

"Charlie, you were really feelin' yourself," said Hylan, continuing to tease.

Taariq jumped into the fray. "I tried to tell you those Air Jordans will get a brother caught up each and every time."

Charlie rolled his eyes. "Ha. Ha. Very funny."

Another round of snickering and elbowing ensued.

After two hours of waiting to see a doctor, Charlie's patience neared an end. He'd almost convinced himself that he would rather go through life with a limp than to sit another minute in the E.R.'s hard plastic chairs.

"Charles Masters?"

"Over here," he called, struggling to his feet.

A shapely Latina nurse smiled when her eyes landed on him. "The doctor can see you now. Would you like for me to get you a wheelchair?"

That was like asking a starving man if he wanted a cracker.

A few minutes later, Consuela, according to her name tag, wheeled him through the crowded hallway behind the reception desk. Getting a room was too much to hope for apparently. Instead, the nurse rolled him behind a makeshift divider and told him that the doctor would see him in a few minutes.

It was another hour.

"Well, well. Sorry to keep you waiting," a voice boomed as the divider was pulled back, which jarred Charlie awake.

"Dr. Weiner?" Charlie asked, startled.

"Ah, Charlie!" A stunned smile spread across his personal physician's face. "What a surprise." He looked down at the paperwork Charlie had filled out at check-in. "I must be tired. I didn't really make a connection when I read your name on the folder."

Charlie squared his shoulders and felt a little better about being in the care of his primary doctor. "I didn't know you worked here at the hospital."

"Well, I fill in from time to time." Dr. Weiner closed the folder and leveled a serious look at Charlie. "You know my office has been trying to reach you."

Charlie instantly recalled the number of messages left on his home answering machine. But with all the trouble going on at the office, he kept putting off returning the doctor's calls. Besides, they probably just wanted to give him the results of his lab work for his upcoming trip.

"Tell you what," Dr. Weiner said after an awkward beat. "Let me take a look at your foot, and let's just have you come into my office in the morning."

"Tomorrow?" Charlie frowned. "Is there something wrong?"

Weiner hesitated again. "I don't have your chart from my office with me, so let's just go over everything then?"

Charlie's gaze lingered on the smiling doctor. He didn't like the sound of that at all.

Chapter 5

Charlie hated doctors. No doubt. His resentment went back to the day he was born, when some heartless doctor smacked him on the butt. Since then, he despised anyone wearing a white coat. Since that first day, medical professionals had put him through an endless ordeal of sharp needles, horrible-tasting prescription medicines, and as he got older, even subjected him to invasive finger-probing in unmentionable areas.

Now with an important business trip to South Africa coming up, Charlie had to deal with a lot of blood work, updating vaccinations and loading up on antibiotics. But it all needed to be done if he was going to save his company.

"Ah, Mr. Masters. You kept your appointment."

Charlie gave an odd-angled smile as he strolled into Dr.

Weiner's office leaning on a cane to protect his sprained ankle. His brain quickly scrolled through his mental Rolodex for the name of the cinnamon-brown beauty at the check-in desk, but luckily he was rescued by her name tag. "Tammy, how are you?"

The roll of her eyes told him she knew he didn't remember her. "So what's the excuse this time? You lost my number? You had another death in the family—the dog, perhaps?"

"I don't own a dog," he said, unruffled by her irritation. He leaned over the counter and smiled into her eyes. "Besides I've been under the weather and have been laid up for a little while."

A spark returned to her disbelieving gaze. "Then maybe I could come over to your place and play nurse?"

"Now that sounds like a plan."

"Humph!"

Charlie glanced over his shoulder and then smiled at the nurse glaring at him. "Ah, Lexi." Embarrassment heated his face. "I didn't see you standing there."

Lexi shook her head. "You'll never change, will you, Charlie?"

He gave her his best puppy dog expression while his smile turned sly. "Can I help flirting when this office is filled with such beautiful women?"

"Sign in right here," Tammy instructed, her lyrical voice now flat.

Determined not to let the women see him sweat, Charlie scribbled his name and handed over his insurance card before Lexi led him to a room to wait for Dr. Weiner. A playboy at heart, Charlie couldn't stop thinking about Tammy's idea of playing nurse—especially if she wore a tight white dress, white fishnet thigh-highs and high-heeled shoes.

Thinking about the fantasy nurse uniform gave Charlie an instant hard-on just as he was sitting down on the doctor's table, giving Lexi a good eyeful.

"Um." She cleared her throat. "The doctor will be with you in a minute."

Charlie nodded and pretended not to notice her distraction as she walked backward. When she bumped into the wall, he gave her a smile.

"Oops," he said.

Lexi jumped and glared at him again before racing out of the room.

He chuckled. Women never failed to amuse him.

Twenty minutes later, when Charlie had just decided to take a quick nap, Dr. Weiner ambled into the room with his thick, black-rimmed glasses sitting on the edge of his nose.

"Ah, Dr. Weiner. Good to see you again," Charlie greeted.

The hunch-shouldered doctor came in with a thin smile and lifted his rheumy eyes toward him. "Afternoon, Charlie."

It was the tone that knotted Charlie's stomach muscles or maybe it was the fact that the chilly room had suddenly grown stuffy. "What is it, Doc?"

Weiner drew in a deep breath and closed the chart in his hand as he pulled up a stool and sat down.

Charlie could literally hear the blood rushing through his veins. He didn't like the look of this. He tried to brace himself the best he could, but he couldn't stop being impatient for the news. "Whatever it is, just tell me. I can handle it," he lied.

The doctor nodded gravely. "Your lab results came in…"

"And…?"

"And… It doesn't look too good." He leveled his serious gaze on Charlie. "You're dying."

Charlie stiffened. "Come again?"

"I know this is coming as a surprise, but the lab results—"

"B-but I feel fine." The doctor's words hit him like an iron fist. It simply wasn't true. It wasn't possible.

Dr. Weiner frowned. "Didn't you tell me two weeks ago that you've been exhausted lately?"

"B-but that's because of work. I've been putting in a lot of hours. I—" Charlie swallowed. "What's wrong with me?"

"It looks like you have aplastic anemia."

"A plastic what?"

"Aplastic anemia. It means you have a low count of all three blood cells. I still need to confirm with a bone marrow test—but with these numbers, I'm pretty sure."

The room roared with silence before the doctor at long last said, "I'm sorry."

Finally finding his courage, Charlie asked, "Okay, how do we treat it?"

The doctor hesitated. "Well, there're a few things we can try—all extremely risky but…."

"How long?" Charlie asked.

"I—I can't just give a date."

"How long?" Charlie insisted.

Dr. Weiner glanced back down at the chart. "Given these numbers, I'd say five to six months, tops."

Chapter 6

"I don't feel right leaving you here like this," Anna complained, setting her suitcase down by the door. "What if something happens while I'm gone?"

"I'm a big girl." Gisella laughed. "I think I can take care of myself."

Anna drew a deep breath. "Nicole and Jade's phone numbers are on the refrigerator. Call them if you need help with anything. I'm leaving to go to my company's headquarters in New York, but I'll call you every day."

"Yes, *Mom*," Gisella sassed, bumping her hip against her sister's before marching out of Anna's bedroom. "Sasha and I will be fine."

Her sister followed her to the kitchen and watched her slip on her Kiss the Chef apron and then pull out a variety of bowls and ingredients from every cabinet. "You really do love doing this stuff, don't you?" she said, folding her arms and leaning against the kitchen's door frame. "You'd live in a kitchen if you could."

"Don't think I haven't thought about it," Gisella joked, measuring out flour and vanilla extract. "I'm still trying to crack *grandmère*'s famous recipe for her *Amour Chocolat*."

"Why don't you just ask her for it?"

"Now *that's* a novel idea." Gisella smacked her palm against her head. "Why didn't I think of it?"

"She won't give it up, eh?"

"She claims the recipe is top-secret because its effects can be dangerous for those who don't respect its power."

"Dangerous?" Anna repeated skeptically. "We're talking about chocolate, right?"

"Ah, but not just any kind of chocolate." Gisella waved a finger at her sister. "There is what you might call a culinary urban legend about *grandmère*'s *Amour Chocolat*. It is said that just one bite of the decadent treat ignites passion."

"What? Like an aphrodisiac? C'mon, people have been saying that about chocolate for years. It's not true."

"But ah! This recipe is the real deal. Trust me. I know."

Anna lifted a single brow. "You've had it before?"

Casting her eyes down, Gisella bit her lower lip and tried her best not to look like a blushing fool.

"Gisella! Don't tell me there's a wild side to you."

"There's a lot you don't know about me," she sassed with a shrug of indifference. "Anyway, I'm no closer figuring out the recipe now than when I first started a couple of years ago, mainly because I have to rely on memory. But I *will* figure it out," she vowed.

"So whose bones did you jump when you ate this magical stuff?"

Gisella's smile faded when her mind tumbled back. "Robert's."

"Oh." Anna sobered. "There I go shoving my foot into my big mouth."

"Don't," Gisella said, waving off the apology. "The past is the past. All I can do is learn from it and move forward and create new memories."

Her sister's eyes narrowed on her. "Do you already have someone else in mind?"

"What? No!" Gisella lied, her face heating up with embarrassment. "I'm just saying that you never know what's in the future. That's all."

"Humph!" As usual, Anna rolled her eyes at Gisella's romantic fancy. "I already know what my future holds—a lot of romance novels and gallons of ice cream."

Gisella laughed guiltily as she turned toward the refrigerator and took out the milk, butter and eggs. "As much fun as that can be, I'd much rather curl up to a warm body at night."

"You'll learn. Men aren't worth half the trouble they cause. All a woman needs to be happy is a great career, some nice toys and a hearty stock of copper-topped batteries. Trust me."

Masters Holdings now operated with a skeletal crew. Commercial and housing construction in Atlanta had slowly ground down to a complete stop in the last four years. While puffed up economists, Wall Street analysts and the same tried-and-true politicians argued whether the nation was in a recession or not, companies like Charlie's were hemorrhaging money at a record pace.

When the first signs of trouble emerged, Charlie foolishly believed that his company could survive an economic slow down. But this was like a financial drought that was on the verge of wiping him out.

Not that it should matter anymore.

Charlie's gaze drifted to his computer inbox and noted the number of messages from Dr. Weiner's office in the last week. He sighed and waffled again over picking up the phone. Why *was* he putting off making the appointment for the bone marrow test?

He leaned forward and put his elbows on the desk. Maybe he just didn't want to know the truth. He didn't know how to go about the business of dying.

How was that for denial.

"Mr. Masters," Jackson Boyett, Charlie's executive assistant chirped over the intercom. "You have a call on line one."

Charlie reached for the receiver, hesitated and then asked. "Who is it?"

"It's your mother."

Charlie's heart dropped. He'd been avoiding his mother's calls like the plague. Though a part of him was feeling incredibly guilty about it, another part of him knew it was vital not to let his mother even suspect that something could be wrong. But Arlene Masters's intuition was always sharp as a tack.

Today was Tuesday, and Charlie and his mother had a

standing Tuesday night date. If she didn't have something planned at the senior center, his mother would usually cook him dinner. What was he going to tell her? What should he tell her? If he told her about his aplastic anemia, he knew she would move into his apartment before the end of the workday.

The real question was, could he fly under the radar of his mother's sixth sense? He stared at the red flashing light on the console, took a deep breath and finally answered the phone.

"Well, if it isn't my favorite girl in the whole world," he said, forcing humor into his voice.

"What's wrong?"

Charlie frowned. This was going to be harder than he thought. "Nothing's wrong."

"Come on, Charles. This is me you're talking to. I used to change your diapers. So trust me when I say I know when there's something wrong."

Charlie rolled his eyes as he leaned his head against the palm of his hand. "Trust me, Mom. Nothing is wrong. You know, it's always busy here at the office. I'm just swamped."

"I hope you're not trying to tell me you're not coming to dinner."

"Of course not. You know how much I look forward to your home-cooked meals."

His mother drew a deep breath, and he could tell she was still trying to detect whether he was being straight with her. "Well, I guess not." In the next second, she became bubbly with excitement. "Anyway, I called because I wanted to tell you that we are going to be trying a new dessert tonight," she said in a singsong tone.

"Oh?"

"Don't worry. It's chocolate. I found this new bakery downtown. You're going to love it."

At precisely seven-thirty, Charlie knocked on his mother's door. Dressed in casual jeans and a royal-blue cotton top, Charlie prepared for the performance of a lifetime. After thinking about it for the past few hours, he finally decided *not* to say anything until he had the results of his bone marrow test—that was, *if* he ever took the test.

As he waited for his mother to answer the door, he wondered what would happen to her if the test confirmed the fatal diagnosis. Given his financial situation, he wouldn't have anything to leave her in his will. He'd never thought about it before, and it seemed unnatural to be thinking about it now. Charlie's smile evaporated a second before his mother opened the door.

"Great, you're on—what's wrong?" she asked.

Charlie realized he'd been caught off guard and quickly chiseled his smile back into place. "Nothing." He leaned forward and planted a kiss against her round cheek. "I was just thinking."

"You sure have been doing an awful lot of that lately."

"You're complaining? I seem to recall you always telling me to think before I act, speak and—"

"All right, all right," she said, rolling her eyes. "Get on in here. I have chicken frying on the stove."

Charlie stepped into his mother's quaint and spotless

apartment and drew in a deep breath. The heavenly aroma of fried chicken filled his nostrils and weakened his knees. Nobody could cook like his mother.

A second later his stomach growled in agreement.

Chuckling, his mother patted his firm stomach. "Sounds like you brought a healthy appetite with you."

"Still complaining?"

"Well, what the heck happened to your foot?" She glanced down at his cane.

"Sprained it playing b-ball with the guys."

She shook her head and frowned. "I swear, you boys." She shook her head and disappeared into the kitchen "Have a seat. Dinner will be ready in a second."

Charlie almost followed her, but knew if he stepped a foot into her kitchen, she would have hissy fit. His mother loved serving him as much as she loved cooking for him. Truth be told, he knew he would be lying if he said that he didn't love how she spoiled him.

Growing up in the heart of Atlanta in the 1970s and '80s wasn't exactly easy for him or his single mom, but they always seemed to manage walking the fine line between poor and broke. It helped a lot that he and Derrick were not only best friends, but so were their mothers. Together the two women kept both boys in line.

Derrick's mother eventually remarried, while Charlie's mother still seemed to mourn the loss of his father.

A sad smile ghosted around Charlie's face as he reflected on his childhood—the good and the bad.

Charlie's gaze floated across the dining room and landed on the multitude of pictures hanging on the wall.

There were pictures of his mother when she was young. Some of his grandparents, and even one of his great-grandmother was smiling back at him. There were plenty of pictures of him, too. Some of them he didn't remember posing for and others that he had fond memories of.

At last his eyes landed on a picture of his parents together. They were teenagers. According to his mother, Jonathan Masters was often mistaken for a white man and as a result of genetics, Charlie had his mother's complexion but his father's eyes.

Jonathan Masters died a young man. He'd gone out on a cold winter's night for baby formula and ended up being an innocent bystander shot dead during a store robbery.

"He was so young," Arlene said, following Charlie's gaze. "There's not a day that goes by that I don't miss him." She looked at Charlie. "I hate that you don't remember him. He would've been so proud of you."

Charlie reached for his mother's hand and gave it a squeeze.

"Despite him dying so young, he lived a full life." She chuckled softly. "Everyone who knew Jonathan knew him to be a good man. Honest. Kind. Loving. And definitely a playboy. You definitely inherited that trait from him."

"What?" Charlie actually blushed. "I don't know what you're talking about."

"Uh-huh." His mother leveled him with a playful look. "I just know Jonathan had so many women beating down his door, his picture should have been in the *Guinness Book of World Records*."

Charlie laughed.

"I'm telling you he had it goin' on. All those girls plotting and scheming. All *I* had to do was invite him over for supper every Sunday. In no time at all I had him eating out of my hand." She glanced down and stared at the gold band still adorning her finger. She sighed. "Now I'm just waiting for you to come to your senses and settle down so I can have me some grandbabies running around here."

Charlie automatically rolled his eyes. "Oh, are we about to have that conversation again?"

"Nope. I'm going into the kitchen and get your food, but don't think I'm going to be around here cooking for you forever. Find you a girl who knows her way around the kitchen instead of the mall, and you'll have yourself a winner."

A few minutes later, his mother set in front of him a large plate piled high with fried chicken, candied yams, collard greens with bits of ham hock and her off-the-chain homemade cornbread.

Charlie looked over at his mother with tears in his eyes. "Have I told you lately how much I love you?"

"You better." Arlene lovingly patted the top of his hand and placed a kiss against his brow.

Charlie grabbed his fork but was quickly smacked on the back of the head.

"Now you know we say grace around here," she reminded him. She eased into her chair, took his hand and bowed her head. "O Lord, we bless thy holy name for this mercy, which we have now received from thy bounty and goodness. Feed now our souls with thy grace, that we may make it our meat and drink to do thy gracious will, through Jesus Christ our savior. Amen."

Arlene lifted her head, but was surprised when Charlie added more to the prayer.

"God of all blessings, source of all life, giver of all grace, we thank You for the gift of life, for the breath that sustains us, and for the food of this earth that nurtures life…"

He paused and Arlene opened her mouth to end with an "Amen" but her son wasn't finished.

"We also want to thank You for the love of family and friends for without which there would be no life…"

Another pause, Arlene opened one eye, waited and then opened her mouth again, only for Charlie to trudge on.

"For these, and all blessings, we give You thanks, eternal, loving God, through Jesus Christ we pray… Amen."

"Amen!" she jumped in and lifted her head to stare wide-eyed at her son.

Charlie shoved a forkful of collards into his mouth and then realized his mother was staring. "What?" he asked after swallowing.

Arlene folded her arms. "Are you sure nothing is wrong with you?"

"I'm sure," Charlie lied again, and shoveled more food into his mouth.

His mother stared.

When dinner was over, Arlene stood and went back into the kitchen and then returned with a red-and-gold cake box.

"Wait until you try this," she said. "I swear this woman could give me a run for my money."

Charlie's eyes widened at the gold script on the center of the box. "Sinful Chocolate," he read, remembering the

French beauty from his surprise birthday party. "Let me guess. Molten chocolate."

His mother's face lit up with surprise. "How did you know?"

"I met the owner."

"Really?" His mother voice registered her surprise. "She's a very attractive woman."

"You don't say," he said, amused.

"I *do* say. And if you asked me, *she's* the kind of woman you should be dating. Beautiful, smart—and if she can cook as well as she can bake—you two would be a match made in heaven."

Chapter 7

"I'm sorry, Mr. Masters, but we cannot approve you for this loan."

Stunned, Charlie blinked at the loan officer across the desk. A few erratic heartbeats later, he finally managed to sputter, "Why?" He straightened in his chair. "I have a triple-A credit rating, my paperwork is in order…"

The attractive dark-skinned beauty smiled. "Your debt to ratio is a major concern, and with this credit crisis we're taking a harder look at our loan applications. Unfortunately, you are what we call high risk at this time."

"High risk? I don't understand. I've never defaulted on a loan, and I've been banking here for over a decade."

The woman's smile remained firmly in place. "Again,

I'm sorry. Maybe once you pay down some of your debt we can help you."

How was it that a bank only wanted to give you money when you didn't need it? After taking a deep breath, Charlie forced himself to relax so he could think clearly. How was he going to make next month's payroll? If he laid off any more people, Masters Holdings would undoubtedly fold before he made his trip overseas.

Sighing, Charlie started to thank the woman for her time when he caught the lazy way she was looking at him. Maybe this was an opening. "Tell you what. Why don't you and I discuss this over dinner?" he suggested.

A new spark lit the woman's eyes. "Dinner?"

Charlie turned on the charm. "I know this wonderful restaurant out in Buckhead. They serve the best seafood in Atlanta. I would be delighted if you could join me."

"Really?"

"Sure. We'll have a nice meal, some wine…" He allowed his sentence to trail off while he gave her a sly smile.

She leaned forward and folded her hands beneath her chin. "And then what?" she inquired huskily.

He shrugged. "Who knows?"

"Maybe you'll take me back to your place?" she suggested. "You'll put on some music, dim the lights and we could dance cheek-to-cheek?"

He smiled.

"Sort of like how we did six years ago when you came in for your last loan?"

Damn. Charlie's face fell. *That's why she looks so familiar.* "Dee."

"Yes, like the little girl from *What's Happening?* What's the matter, you stopped playing your little name game?"

Charlie coughed and then choked over the proverbial foot he'd just shoved into his mouth. "I think I better go," he croaked, reaching for his cane and suitcase.

"You damn right," she snapped.

He climbed to his feet. "Have a good day."

"It's the best damn day I've had in six years."

Charlie couldn't get out of there fast enough. He just hoped he could make it out before she caused a scene. Still wearing a plastic smile, Charlie limped across the bank as fast as could.

"Charlie!"

He kept going.

"Charlie!"

He heard the clatter of heels racing behind him but before he could push through the bank's glass doors, a hand landed on his wrist and pulled.

"Wait, Charlie."

He finally recognized the voice and turned. "Isabella."

She smiled up at him while she tried to catch her breath. "Didn't you hear me calling you?"

"Oh, I—I, uh, guess I was a little distracted," he covered and then glanced over her shoulder to see Dee with her arms crossed and glaring at him from the door of her office.

"You remember Gisella, don't you?" Isabella asked.

He turned in time to see Gisella approach from his right. A new and more genuine smile caressed Charlie's lips. "I most certainly do," he said, holding out his hand. *"Bonjour, mademoiselle."*

"*Bonjour.* We meet again." Gisella slid her silky hand into his, and he felt a stirring in the pit of his stomach while his heart hammered against his rib cage.

"I haven't seen you since you disappeared from my birthday party before I could finish thanking you."

"Well, you looked a little *occupied* with your impressive fan club."

"Oh, that's all the time." Isabella laughed.

Charlie cringed. Surely his best friend's wife wasn't about to throw salt in his game. Not with this woman. Please, God, not with this woman.

"So what are you two doing here?" he asked, hoping to change the subject.

"We're about to become business partners," Isabella boasted. "Isn't that right, Gisella?"

"*Oui.*" Gisella nodded. "*Ma nouvelle amie* here seems to think my little *chocolat* shop has quite a future ahead of it."

Charmed by her accent, Charlie's smile widened.

"I have to agree. I had another one of your cakes for dessert last night. It turns out my mother is also a fan. And trust me, that's a rarity."

"Then tell your mother I said *merci.*"

Charlie couldn't stop staring. He couldn't get over just how absolutely stunning she was.

"Sooo what are you doing here?" Isabella asked.

Charlie continued to stare and smile.

"Charlie?" Isabella snapped her fingers in front of his face and broke his trance.

"What? Oh!" He blinked. "I, uh, was just here on business."

"What is it that you do?" Gisella inquired.

"I own a commercial development construction company." *Just barely.*

"Oh." Gisella nodded. "Impressive." She glanced down. "And what happened to your foot?"

"Oh, it's nothing. It's just a minor sprain from playing basketball with the fellahs." From the corner of Charlie's eyes, he saw Dee break away from her office door and march toward them.

Trouble, Charlie Masters. Trouble.

A wave of panic washed over him, telling him it was definitely time to take his leave. "Well, I gotta go. Itwasa-pleasuretomeetyouagain. Wemustdoitagainsometime," he said hurriedly and turned to leave.

"What? Wait, Charlie," Isabella said, grabbing him again. "I was just about to ask you to join us for lun—"

"Excuse me, ladies," Dee interrupted.

Charlie groaned as he caught the mischievous glint in Dee's eye.

"Are you two friends of Mr. Masters?"

Isabella frowned.

"If not, I only wanted to warn you that he's nothing but a low-down, lying, sex-crazed egomaniac that some vet needs to put out of his misery to save unsuspecting women from being nothing but notches on his bedpost."

Isabella was stunned speechless.

Gisella's eyes widened but then just as quickly seem to twinkle with amusement.

"And on *that* note," Charlie said, clearing his throat and barely holding on to his smile. "I'll be leaving." *Before I catch a case*. He turned and finally strode out of the bank, completely humiliated.

By the time Charlie made it to his Aston Martin V8 Roadster in the parking deck across from the bank, he was wishing he could go back home and start the day all over again. He slid in behind the wheel and then slumped his head back against the headrest. "You're losing your cool, Charlie," he mumbled. What happened to the days when being a playa was fun? Where did this rash of disgruntled lovers come from all of a sudden?

The problem with playing the field too long is that you forget names and faces. It was getting harder and harder to keep them straight and apparently to keep them happy. He replayed the incident in the bank's lobby again in his mind and was convinced that if he ever had the slightest chance of hooking up with Gisella it was completely erased now.

Just then, Isabella and Gisella marched around the bank's corner and headed toward the parking deck. They were laughing and shaking their heads. Hell, he didn't blame them. No doubt Dee's tirade gave them plenty to laugh about.

His eyes locked on to Gisella, and from the safety of his car he was free to just watch the French beauty. It was a cool spring day, and Gisella wore an amazing sky blue wrap dress that hugged her perfect hourglass figure. Hands down, she had the sexiest walk he'd ever seen. As her hips swayed, her breasts jiggled slightly and her onion-shaped bottom simply hypnotized.

"Where, oh where have you been all my life," he whispered.

Isabella said something and Gisella's face lit up and her musical laughter floated across the parking deck. He cocked his head with a lazy smile and continued to watch as her hair billowed in the gentle breeze. His eyes then zeroed in on her full lips and he felt that stirring in the pit of his stomach again while his erection throbbed against his leg.

The two women reached Isabella's red Mercedes, and he had to swallow his disappointment when Gisella disappeared from view. A few heartbeats later, he was shaking his head and telling himself he needed to change the direction of his thoughts. The last thing he needed to be thinking about is getting involved with another woman.

No matter how beautiful.

What was the point? He might have less than six months...

Isabella's Mercedes pulled out of its parking space then disappeared onto Fourteenth Street. After taking a few more deep breaths, Charlie's erection softened, and his heartbeat returned to normal. He started the car and backed up only a few inches when a thumping noise caught his attention. Shifting the car back into Park, Charlie climbed out of his car.

At first he thought that something must be wrong with his vision. But after blinking several times, he knew his eyes weren't playing tricks on him, and he was staring at two flat tires. Then something else caught his eyes. He stepped forward and noticed the hood where someone had keyed in the word *asshole*.

"Great," he groaned. "Just great."

Chapter 8

Saturday morning, Charlie strolled through the doors of Herman's Barbershop with his cane and smiled at the usual suspects as they chimed, "Yo, Charlie!"

"Morning, everybody," he greeted.

Herman Keillor, a tall robust man who was cruising toward his mid-seventies, had owned the busy shop for over forty years. Most of the guys filtered through to hear Herman's stories, tough love advice and sharp haircuts.

Charlie and Derrick had been going to the shop since they were six years old. The other Kappa brothers started coming on their recommendation.

"Right on time," Herman's voice boomed across the room. "I swear, Charlie. That's why you're one of my favorite customers. You don't believe in any of the CP time like the rest of these knuckleheads up in here," he lectured on the sly.

As usual the men just laughed and waved the old barber off. Mounted high in the left corner, a twenty-seven-inch television screen was tuned in to Sportscenter.

"Come on over," Herman directed. "I've got your seat all warmed up and ready for you."

Charlie made his way across the shop and eased into the leather chair.

Men in the neighborhood filtered in and out daily, but Saturday had always been Herman's busiest day of the week. Six barbers ranging from old school to new school donned burgundy barber jackets with Herman's name scrawled across the back. For an old redbrick building, the shop still managed to look modern and brand-new.

"So what's been happening, Charlie?" Herman asked, smiling and draping a black smock around his neck.

Charlie hesitated a moment and then answered with his tried and true. "You know the drill. Same ole, same ole."

"Same crap, different day, huh?"

"You got it."

Herman's was the place to be to discuss women, politics and sports. The perfect place for men to just be themselves, to get and give advice and just plain bond with one another.

"I hear you had an off-the-chain birthday party," said Bobby, Herman's nineteen-year-old great-grandson, who was sitting in the leather chair across from him. Like everyone else in the shop, Charlie had watched Bobby move from sweeping up the floors to trying his hand at being a weekend barber.

"Yeah. It was pretty cool."

"Well, what does a young brother gotta do to cop an invite?" Bobby asked, pretending to be hurt by the exclusion.

"Are you kidding me? You're a college man now. Why the heck would you want to hang out with us? I'm sure there are plenty of honeys around you 24-7."

Bobby blushed while a sly smile hooked across his face. "Honeys? Man, you *are* old school."

"Lawd, Lawd," Herman mumbled, reaching for his clippers. "What you need to do is forget about those fast girls and put your nose deeper into those books."

"Relax, Gramps." Bobby smiled. "I got it all covered like Allstate."

Charlie laughed. It seemed like it was just yesterday that Bobby was pencil-thin with thick, black-rimmed glasses and a face covered in acne. Now, he'd filled out and his skin had cleared up and he was flexin' his playa's card. "You still pledging Kappa Psi Kappa?" Charlie asked.

"You know it."

The bell jingled above the shop's door and Taariq and Hylan entered the shop. After a round of perfunctory "Yo, whassup," Taariq and Hylan made it over to Charlie's chair to exchange a couple of knuckle bumps.

"What's happening, captain?" Taariq asked, grinning.

"You got it," Charlie said.

"You gonna let me hook you up today, Taariq?" Bobby asked, getting up out of his chair and gesturing for Taariq to take a seat.

For a full year now, Bobby had been harassing everyone who came in the barbershop, trying to build up his clientele by siphoning off Herman's loyal customers.

Taariq stared him down while he wrestled with his decision. "Man, if you jack this up it's gonna be just you and me out back."

Bobby beamed a smile at him and patted the leather chair. "Have a seat."

There was a round of snickering, all of them probably thinking that Taariq was being incredibly brave, seeing as how just two months ago Bobby shaved a bald spot in the middle of J. T. Caesar's hair because he'd gotten distracted by a thick romp shaker in a BET rap video.

"Better you than me," Hylan said, shaking his head.

"You ain't never lied," J.T. agreed with a flash of his front gold tooth. "Yo, yo, Hylan. I got that new Jay-Z underground joint. Five dollars."

"That's all right," Hylan chuckled.

"What about some DVDs? I already got that new Will Smith joint."

"C'mon, man. You know I don't buy none of that bootleg crap."

"What about some socks?" He opened his jacket and pulled out a massive bundle.

"What the hell?" Hylan asked. "Has anybody *ever* bought socks from you?"

"Yeah, man. That's my hottest selling item."

Charlie laughed. This place was just where he needed to be to forget about his troubles.

"Oh, by the way," Taariq said, returning his attention to Charlie. "I rushed that paint job for you. You can come by the shop any time and pick it up."

"Thanks, man. I owe you one."

"Uh-huh. Word around town is that you're starting to have women trouble lately. Vandalism, causing a scene at the bank—"

Charlie groaned. "How did you find out?"

"Isabella told Derrick, Derrick told me, and then I told everybody I could think of." He laughed.

"Thanks, dawg."

"Don't mention it."

Charlie suffered a few jeers.

Hylan rocked on his heels. "Losing your touch, ain't ya?"

"Say it ain't so!" Bobby said, wrapping a smock around Taariq's neck. "I thought it was a sad day when pimp number one went down. Don't tell me that the replacement has lost his Midas touch."

"I take it you mean Derrick. And we're not pimps."

"Whatever. I just know the faster you old-school playas get out the game, the more *honeys* there will be for me."

Everybody roared at that.

"Man, if you don't get your rookie butt outta here," Taariq said. "You still got breast milk on your breath and you up in here thinking you a real playa."

Bobby's face darkened with embarrassment. "C'mon now. Stop frontin'."

"Yeah, man," Hylan stepped in and corrected Taariq. "He's been grown for at least two weeks."

The guys cracked up again, including Herman.

The shop's bell rang again and Stanley strolled inside with his customary wide smile. None of the regulars called the lanky redhead by his first name. Instead, they affectionately called Stanley "Breadstick" and sometimes "Whitey," probably because Stanley was the only white man to get his hair cut at Herman's.

"Yo, everybody, whassup?" Stanley greeted, acting more black than everybody else. At this point, everyone was used to it and welcomed him into the fold just the same.

"I know one thing," Bobby said. "I'm getting more action than *this* dude."

There was another roar of laughter, and Stanley tried to play off his confusion by laughing along with everyone else.

Herman shook his head. "Boys still playing at being men."

The guys pretended not to hear him, but in no time Herman felt like preaching. "You know ya'll need to take a page out of your friend Derrick's book."

Right on cue, the bell rang again and Derrick entered the shop.

"Speaking of the devil," Hylan said and waited as Derrick made his way over to them.

Derrick tossed everyone a slow nod.

"Now this one finally got it right and settled down," Herman said, pointing a firm finger at Derrick.

"Whoa. Whoa. What did I miss?"

"I was about to tell your friends about how nothing good can come from playing the field with all these different women. One of these days you're gonna roll up on the wrong one. Charlie already got one vandalizing his car. He's just one step away from taking a hot grits shower. If you don't believe me, ask Al Green."

"Who?" Bobby asked.

"Lawd, Lawd, please help these knuckleheads running around here—starting with my own."

Charlie smiled. Once Herman got started there was no stopping him.

"I'm going to agree with Herman," Derrick said.

Charlie and the rest of the Kappa brothers rolled their eyes. Derrick had been siding with Herman ever since he'd said 'I do'.

"Be still," Herman warned Charlie and then clicked back on his trimmers.

"For real," Derrick said, easing his hands into his pockets and rocking on his heels next to Hylan. "I don't regret a single moment once I finally turned in my playa's card."

"That's right." The trimmers were clicked off again. "There's nothing better than the love of one special woman. A man needs peace in his house—in his life."

"Yeah, yeah, yeah." Taariq droned, unconvinced.

"Mark my words. You learn sooner or later."

Herman's speech stayed with Charlie for the rest of the day while he thought about his past relationships. And there were a lot. With the clock ticking maybe it was time he tried to set things right.

There's nothing better than the love of one special woman.

Each time Herman's voice repeated those words, Gisella floated to the forefront of his mind. But just as quickly, he would shake off the image. That avenue was closed. If Dr. Weiner's diagnosis held, then the last thing he needed to be starting was a relationship. He needed to start focusing on making peace with his past.

As Charlie made it back to his apartment building, his thoughts muddled together. Tonight, he would pull out his thick little black book and start making some calls. Hell, it just might take him the whole six months to call them all.

When Charlie slipped his key into the apartment door and stepped inside, he received another shock of his life. Sucking in a breath, his eyes roamed across busted furniture, shattered glass and the word *asshole* scrawled across his white walls in red spray paint.

"Who in the hell is this chick?"

Chapter 9

Gisella's business was booming.

Word of mouth from Charlie's surprise birthday party continued to spread like wild fire. And now Waqueisha kept calling with outrageously large orders to fill for people in Atlanta's entertainment industry.

After running around like a chicken with its head cut off, she realized that she did need help and took Isabella up on her offer.

"Trust me," Isabella boasted. "By this time next year, Ms. Winfrey will be naming your chocolates as one of her favorite things."

Smiling, Gisella shook her head. "When you dream, you dream big, don't you?"

"You just concentrate on making your wonderful treats, and leave the business end to me."

Gisella drew a deep breath and resolved to do just that. The two new business partners huddled together over her sister's dining-room table and discussed everything from hiring more help to balancing their budget. The task was made a little difficult with Sasha constantly jumping on the table and waiting to be petted.

Finally, around ten o'clock, Derrick started blowing up Isabella's cell phone and urging her to come home.

On his fourth call, Gisella smiled at her new partner. "We better call it night," Gisella said.

Isabella agreed, though it was clear she was still excited about this latest career change. "I'll see you bright and early at the shop," she said, giving Gisella a final hug at the door.

When she turned to leave, Gisella could no longer ignore the anxious knot looping in her stomach. "Um…"

Isabella stopped with her hand frozen on the door. "Yes?"

Suddenly feeling foolish, Gisella shifted her weight nervously from side to side. "I was wondering if, um, you heard from Charlie again."

A single brow inched higher towards the center of Isabella's forehead. "Not since we saw him at the bank Friday."

Gisella nodded and swallowed the lump in the center of her throat.

"Why?" Isabella pressed.

Unable to stop the heat from rushing into her face, Gisella's brain short-circuited while she tried to come up with a sufficient excuse for her inquiry. When all she could manage was to bump her gums in silence, a knowing smile eased across Isabella's face.

"You like him, don't you?"

No. Just say no. "He's…interesting."

Isabella snickered. "I think that's putting it mildly—especially after that weird episode at the bank."

"Well, you definitely gave that loan officer a good piece of your mind," Gisella said, laughing.

"After I'd finally recovered from my shock. Poor Charlie. I just know he was humiliated."

"Well." Gisella tilted her head, hedging. "Are we sure that he didn't deserve it? I mean…I've heard rumors."

Isabella drew a deep breath and Gisella thought that maybe she shouldn't be questioning her about a friend. "I'm sorry. I shouldn't have—I mean, forget I said anything."

"No. No. It's fine," Isabella assured her. "I mean… Charlie does have quite a reputation. A lot of it is true, unfortunately." She took another breath. "Of course, Derrick had the same reputation, too, before we met."

Gisella nodded and remembered the covetous glances women made toward the handsome Derrick Knight at the party. She also remembered how he only had eyes for his wife. "You're a lucky woman."

"I am," Isabella agreed, blushing. "There's not a morning I don't wake up and pinch myself."

Gisella relished finding another hopeless romantic. "My sister seems to think there aren't any good single men out here anymore. She's given up."

Isabella cocked her head. "What about you?"

"Me?" Gisella echoed.

"Yeah, you. Has your ex turned you off to finding true love?"

"Tell her," Fantasy Charlie whispered against her ear.

"No." Gisella cleared her throat. "Of course not."

Fantasy Charlie chuckled and brushed a kiss against the back of her neck.

"Good," Isabella said. "I'm glad to hear it. I truly believe that if I could find true love, then surely someone as beautiful as you should have no problem."

Gisella frowned at the odd comment.

"And don't let the rumors about Charlie dissuade you."

"You should listen to the girl." Fantasy Charlie moved next to Isabella and folded his arms.

"Charlie is like a big kid. A lot of the women he's dated act like little girls. They just keep putting his favorite toys in front of him and then act shocked when someone with newer or bigger toys lures him away."

"She has an interesting way of putting things," Charlie said.

Gisella giggled.

Isabella smiled. "What I mean is, Charlie will act more like a man when he meets a real woman. Does that make sense?"

Fantasy Charlie shook his head. *"No."*

"It makes perfect sense," Gisella answered and then gave Isabella another departing hug. "I'll see you in the morning."

After Isabella left the apartment, Gisella closed the door and slumped back against it.

"I thought she would never leave," Fantasy Charlie said, easing up to her and brushing a kiss along her neck. *"What do you say we go back to the bedroom and have a little fun?"*

Gisella glanced up at him, thinking over Isabella's words about the real Charlie being a big kid. "Not tonight. I have a headache."

"Do you know anyone who'd want to do this to you, sir?" Officer Todd asked, with his notepad and pen in hand.

"Not off the top of my head," Charlie grumbled and massaged his throbbing temples. He took another hard look around his ransacked apartment and felt the blood boil in his veins.

"You said that you filed another police report yesterday about your car being vandalized?"

Charlie nodded and couldn't help but feel he'd been cast into some pathetic B-movie horror flick.

Officer Todd frowned. "Are you sure you can't think of anyone, sir? Perhaps an ex-wife or old girlfriend…or boyfriend?"

"What?"

"Sorry—but we never know. Since nothing was stolen, clearly this was a crime of passion."

Charlie flashed the man an irritated glare. "I'm not gay, and I've never been married."

"And your old girlfriends?" the officer asked undaunted.

"That's obviously a different matter," Charlie said, exhaling a long breath, racing through a list in his mind. When no woman stood out in his mind, a painful throbbing at his temples began to hammer double time. "I'll have to get back to you on that one."

"All right." Officer Todd scribbled a few more notes on

his notepad and then handed Charlie a card. "Just give us a call if you're able to think of anything else."

"Sure thing." Charlie slid the card into his pocket and then held the door open while the officer and his partner made their exit. Once they were gone, he shut the door and took another disheartening look at the damage before him.

With no other choice, Charlie rolled up his sleeves and got busy cleaning. Hours later, he gave up and decided the job was going to require real professionals. Close to midnight he limped over to the bar and found one unbroken bottle of Jack Daniels and poured himself a drink.

It took three before he was completely relaxed.

"An ex-girlfriend or boyfriend." He laughed. Hell, what else was he going to do? As he continued to survey the damage, he reflected over his cavalier lifestyle and the numerous one-night stands. Up until now, he'd viewed it all as harmless fun. He'd never made or broken any promises, nor had he asked for any in return. He always made sure his dates had a great time, and then they were free to go on their merry separate ways.

Maybe he had been too naive.

Charlie stood up from the bar and hobbled to his bedroom—another disaster area. At least he was able to clear off a space on the bed so he'd have some place to sleep tonight. He reached underneath the mattress and hoped what he was searching for was still there. He panicked for a moment, but then his hand finally brushed against the spine of a book.

Smiling, Charlie set his whiskey down on the night-stand and pulled out his thick little black book. Such a book was the hallmark of every true playa. His didn't just contain the names and numbers of the beautiful women who'd been so gracious with their time and bodies, but also notes and a very intricate rating system he'd conjured up in high school.

The book was his most treasured possession.

He flipped through the pages, and a flutter of memories danced before his eyes. If the good Lord did decide his time was up, Charlie realized he'd lived one hell of a life—just not a complete one.

Charlie's smile disappeared as a lump of regret clogged his throat and reality hit him hard. Obviously, he had broken a few hearts over the years, and if he was facing the end of his life maybe he should be using this time to right a few wrongs.

He returned to the first page of his black book and read the first name—Abby. "Three and a half stars." That wasn't too bad, he thought and picked up the phone.

As he dialed, he thought briefly about what he would say. He drew a blank while the line rang but before he could hang up, a woman answered.

"Hello."

"Uh, hello." He clutched the phone. "Is, um, Abby there?"

"This is she."

"Oh, Abby." He cleared his throat and tried to control a wave of panic. "This is, um, Charlie—Charlie Masters. You probably don't remember me—"

"Charlie Masters!" She perked up. "Oh, my God. I can't believe it's you."

He smiled at the reception. Maybe this won't be so hard after all.

"My goodness." She sighed. "How have you been?"

"Not so good. I'm dying." He blurted and then smacked a hand across his forehead.

"What?"

"That didn't come out right."

"You mean…" She gasped.

Charlie immediately knew she'd jumped to the wrong conclusion. "No. No. No. No. It's not what you thinking," he rushed to say. "I don't have a sexually transmitted disease," he stressed. "It's not that at all."

"What, then?" she asked, obviously confused. "Is it cancer?"

"No." He exhaled again and felt his migraine return. "It's aplastic anemia."

"It's a plastic what?"

"It's just a rare form of anemia."

The line fell silent.

"Hello? Are you there?"

"Oookay," she said hesitantly. "Sooo, why are you calling?"

"Well." He cleared his throat. "I was doing a lot of thinking, and I wanted apologize for, uh…" He looked down at his notes in the book. "Standing you up that time."

"You mean…senior prom?"

Charlie frowned and squinted down at the book. Apparently his intricate system didn't include dates. "Yeah, well. Again…sorry."

There was another long silence.

"So, I'll let you go. It was nice talking to you." He quickly disconnected the call. "Real smooth," he said, rolling his eyes and reaching for his drink again.

Still, he thought after a moment, it didn't go too bad. He probably just needed to tighten up his speech a bit and try to just concentrate on the women outside of high school.

Charlie glanced at the clock and realized that it was getting late. He picked up the book again. Tomorrow he would call Allison…and Anna.

Chapter 10

"Is this some kind of joke?" Allison asked, frowning at him over her Belgian waffle.

Charlie glanced around the Georgia Diner, smiled at a few people he suspected were eavesdropping and shifted uncomfortably in his seat. "No. It's no joke," he said, praying there wouldn't be an explosion. He had no idea what possessed him to do this in person. It might have had a lot to do with the fact that he'd generally liked Allison. Once he remembered who she was.

They'd met in a public library. She had her nose buried in a mystery book. He was struggling with a term paper.

Allison was kind and nurturing. However, she was also a tad bit clingy and had a habit of laughing like a hyena.

"You mean you weren't a secret agent for the CIA?"

Oh, yeah…she was a little gullible, too.

"Sorry," he said, cringing. "I'm afraid not."

"What about that elaborate story about a covert mission to bring down the Hawaiian Mafia in New Jersey?"

Hawaiian Mafia? "Never been to New Jersey."

Allison lowered her fork and eased back in her chair. "So, what? I'm supposed to feel sorry for you because *now* you're about to kick the bucket? Is that it?"

"Not exactly." He shifted in his chair. "I just want to apologize and bring closure if you thought that I've done anything to—"

"Unbelievable!" Allison crossed her arms. "The only reason I slept with you was because I thought I had a patriotic and civil duty. You *said* you were leaving for a top secret mission in Mauritania and that you may not survive. I thought you were dead for the last fourteen years?"

Charlie cocked his head, thinking she was taking this a bit too far. "C'mon. That is *not* why you slept with me."

Allison rolled her eyes, but a smile teased the corners of her lips. "So what's the play this time? You have six months to live, and now you want me to take you back to my place for one last fling?"

Leaning his elbow on the table, Charlie pinched the bridge of his nose. "No. That's not it."

"Oh," she said, disappointment clearly in her tone. "Would you like to go back to my apartment?"

He frowned. "Aren't you married now?"

"Marcus doesn't get out on parole until next month."

"Uh, thanks, but…I'll pass."

Allison shrugged. "Can't blame a girl for trying."

* * *

Charlie's relationship with Anna was complicated. Even though they'd never dated or were intimate, Anna was perhaps the closest female friend he'd ever had. To him, she was like a sister—smart and easygoing. They met at a frat party back when he attended Morehouse and she the neighboring Spelman College. A friend of hers, Nicole something-or-another, had too much to drink and was unable to drive and Anna had never driven a stick shift.

Charlie and Taariq stepped forward and helped her out by driving them back to their dorms. It was the beginning of a nice friendship, especially when he discovered that she was a whiz in calculus. Unfortunately, their relationship was derailed a year later when Charlie grew interested in her new roommate Roxanne.

Roxanne had the hottest body on campus, and Charlie was just one in a long line trying to hook up with her. For an advantage, he started milking Anna for information about her roommate—on the sly. When he started seeing Roxanne, he kept it from Anna…until she caught them in bed together.

It wasn't until she was crying and cussing him out did he realize that Anna's feelings for him went beyond friendship.

She accused Charlie of using her.

And he had—unintentionally.

She never spoke to him again.

Anna's old number was no longer in service. Charlie spent an hour at his apartment Googling and searching the white pages online for an address. If there was one woman he truly wanted to make peace with it was Anna. As it turned out, he was in luck. She still lived in Atlanta, not too far from his downtown office.

Once Charlie wrote down the new address, he stared at it, contemplating. Did he really want to do this? Finally, he stood, folded the paper and slipped it into his pocket.

"Ah, this is the life," Gisella sighed, sinking deep into her bubble bath. She had waited all week for this. Sunday was the only day the shop was closed and she could use some R & R. She was determined to do absolutely nothing. With Anna still out of town, Gisella had the apartment all to herself. She could run around naked if she wanted. A tempting thought.

The first and only thing on her schedule was to pamper herself, which was why she'd borrowed one of her sister's romance books, globbed on a thick cucumber mask and poured a big glass of wine.

Fantasy Charlie showed up for a few minutes, but she quickly sent him away. After all, there was plenty of time to play with him later.

In no time, the stress of the past week seeped out of her body, and she fell fast asleep. When she awoke, the bubbles were gone, and the water was cold. Laughing, she climbed out of the tub with her fingers and toes nearly pickled and with the real challenge of removing the cucumber mask that had hardened into green concrete.

It took a lot of scrubbing, but when she was through, her skin was as soft and smooth as a newborn baby's. After blow-drying the ends of her hair, she hummed her way into her bedroom for some underwear, rubbed her favorite lotions into her skin and then danced to the kitchen for a big bowl of cereal.

No cooking today.

Still dancing, she scanned her sister's music collection. When she found an old 1980s classic, Gisella slipped the disc into the CD player and turned the volume up to full blast.

Charlie walked into the brownstone, puzzled by the sound of Deniece Williams's "Let's Hear It for the Boy" blaring out into the hallway. Was there a 1980s retro reunion party going on? When he realized that the music was coming from the apartment number written on his paper, he began to have second thoughts about this whole thing.

"All right, Charlie. Let's just get this over with," he coached, drawing a deep breath. He knocked on the door and waited. When it was clear no one heard him, he rang the bell and knocked again.

Still no answer.

He thought to wait for the song to fade, but it immediately launched into Kenny Loggins's "Footloose."

Now, he started hammering and shouting, "Hello!"

As a last ditch effort, he tried the door and was surprised to find it unlocked. He paused for a moment, then slowly turned the knob. "Hello!" He entered the apartment.

Kenny Loggins continued to cut loose as Charlie inched further into the apartment.

"Hello! Anybody?"

Charlie rounded a corner and faced the living room. He stopped in his tracks. There, in all her Victoria's Secret glory, danced an ebony goddess holding an orange cat. The ability to speak or even to process thought grinded to a halt. Surely, he looked like a cartoon with his mouth hanging open and his tongue rolling onto the floor.

Gisella jiggled and wiggled and really got into the old movie soundtrack. She was completely clueless of Charlie's presence, much less how his erection was trying to steeple like an Egyptian pyramid in his pants.

Forget six months, Charlie had died and gone to heaven the moment he'd entered this apartment.

Then something incredible happened. Gisella turned around and flashed him a smile.

"Hello, lover," she singsonged playfully.

Charlie looked over his shoulder to make sure she was talking to him.

She was.

To his surprise, she danced and bopped her way toward him with a sly smile and the unmistakable glint of seduction in her eyes.

Hot damn. This is my lucky day.

When she was within inches of him, the scent of strawberries swirled around his senses, making him light-headed…and incredibly horny.

"How about a kiss?" she asked.

Before he could answer, she planted her full breasts against his chest and swept her sweet tongue inside his mouth. He moaned and started to wrap his arms around her waist when she suddenly jerked back and screamed.

Chapter 11

One should never scream while holding a cat.

The minute Sasha's nails dug into Gisella's arm, she was airborne. When the startled cat landed on Charlie, she turned into a weapon of mass destruction.

Charlie roared.

Sasha shrieked.

And Gisella screamed and ran from the room. "Oh, my God. Oh, my God," she chanted, slamming her bedroom door behind her. To calm down, she paced the floor and fanned herself. "That didn't just happen," she mumbled. "It didn't. It couldn't have." She rolled her eyes skyward. "Oh, God, please say that didn't happen."

She started praying in French.

Unfortunately, Charlie and Sasha's continued war prevented her from sinking into denial. Gulping in a few deep breaths, she raced over to her chest of drawers and slung clothes around until she found a pair of sweatpants and a white T-shirt. Once she was dressed, she still hesitated to leave her room. What was she going to say? How could she explain kissing him like that?

And damn. What a kiss.

Just thinking of it caused her heart to speed up again. Who on earth would ever believe that she kissed him because she thought he was a figment of her imagination?

Suddenly, the apartment was quiet.

Gisella inched toward the door. Was Sasha safe? Didn't someone say something about not trusting Charlie alone with anything with breasts and a pulse? Slowly, Gisella pressed her ear against the door.

Silence.

Did he leave?

She closed her eyes, held her breath and strained to hear the slightest sound.

"Gisella, are you in there?" came Charlie's low baritone.

She leaped from the door.

His tone was barely above a whisper, but it had the effect of an excited cheerleader shouting through a megaphone.

"Gisella?"

"Um." She hesitated. "What are you doing here?"

"Look. I knocked, but you had the music turned up so loud you wouldn't have heard a bomb going off." He chuckled.

"Oh," she said, unprepared for a logical explanation. But on second thought, that only answered why he was *inside* the apartment, not why he'd come there in the first place.

"Actually, I was looking for a friend."

She frowned. They were hardly friends. Hell, they barely qualified as acquaintances. "I never gave you this address," she said, still weary about opening her door.

"You didn't. I looked up the address on the Internet."

Okay. Was he a stalker?

"Why would you look me up on the Internet?"

"Oh. No. Not you," he rushed to explain. "No. I was looking for an old *college* friend, Anna Jacobs. Wait. Isn't Jacobs your last name?"

Charlie and Anna were old college friends? Gisella snatched opened the door and Sasha darted in between her legs with a loud meow.

However, the *real* war victim was clearly Charlie.

"*Mon Dieu.* Look at you!" Her eyes widened at the number of scratches covering his face, neck and arms. "Come here." She grabbed him by the wrist and led him toward her adjoining bedroom. "Here. Take a seat." She lowered the toilet seat and then rustled for some supplies.

Charlie sat and looked around. "I'm sure it's not as bad as it looks," he said.

"Nonsense," she said. "You're bleeding." Gisella twisted open a bottle of alcohol and pulled out a few cotton balls. "Now this is going to sting a bit."

Despite the warning, Charlie sucked in a shocked breath and bounced around on the toilet seat like a Mexican jumping bean.

"Be still," she instructed softly and then blew on a few deep gashes. "Is that better?"

Charlie grew still. "A little."

Gisella glanced up and their eyes locked. "You're a big baby, no?"

His cheeks dimpled. "I wouldn't say that."

For a few seconds, the bathroom tiles magnified their shallow breathing and Gisella swore it even picked up the sound of her heartbeat. Fantasy Charlie paled in comparison to the real deal. Charlie Masters could easily grace the glossy pages of fashion magazines instead of wheeling and dealing behind some office desk. He was just that beautiful.

Forcing herself out of her self-imposed trance, she returned her attention to cleaning a few more scratches, especially the long one across his right cheek. When she leaned forward, Lord help her, she could literally feel his warm breath rush against the exposed portion of her cleavage in her low-cut tee. It took every ounce of her willpower to keep her knees from buckling and depositing her on his lap. All the while, his gaze remained locked on her.

"I'm beginning to think you're a masochist."

She blinked. "A what?"

"Someone who enjoys torturing people." When she still looked confused, he added, "Either kiss me again or let me stand up."

She quickly backed away from him.

"I thought so." He stood and eyed a Band-Aid in the corner of the medicine cabinet. "May I?"

She nodded, swallowing the lump amassing in her throat.

Charlie leaned toward the mirror and applied an invisible band-aid against his cheek. "There. Good as new."

She smiled. "Sorry I threw Sasha at you."

"Sorry I frightened you."

They stood staring at each other, but Gisella knew what they were both thinking about.

That kiss.

"So," she said, hoping to deter him from asking about it. "How do you know my sister?"

He stepped back. "Anna is your sister?"

"Half sister," she corrected. "Different mothers, same father."

Charlie blinked. "Oh. I would have never thought— you two don't look anything alike."

That was true. Anna was tall and angular and Gisella was thick and curvy. Though both women were attractive, the facial features were stark opposites.

"Well, I take it she's not here." He laughed. "Know when she'll be home?"

"Actually, she's out of town for a couple of weeks. In the meantime, it's just me and Sasha."

"The killer cat."

Gisella laughed.

"Well," he said with a note of disappointment.

"When she calls," Gisella said, "I'll be happy to tell her you came by."

"That'll be great." Charlie bobbed his head and went back to staring at her. The memory of their kiss still threatened to become a topic of discussion.

"Do you want to leave a number so she can call you back?" Gisella offered.

"Sure. Um, you gotta pen?"

Gisella glanced around and decided against using a tube

of lipstick to write a message. "There should be one up front," she said, leading the way.

As they walked back through her bedroom, Sasha curled into a ball on the edge of Gisella's bed and meowed at Charlie as he walked by.

"I don't think Killer cares for me much."

"She'll be all right." In the living room, Gisella found pen and paper.

Charlie jotted down his name and cell phone number and handed it over. After another beat of silence, he said, "I still can't believe you two are sisters."

"We have been all my life," she joked.

They stared at each other as if waiting for the other person to bring up the taboo subject. It was going to be a long wait if it was up to Gisella.

As if reading her thoughts, Charlie nodded and finally took his first step toward the door. "I guess I'll let you get back to your…uh, dancing."

Gisella's embarrassment rushed back. "Oh, I can't believe you saw that."

Charlie stopped and loitered for a few more seconds. "You have some pretty good moves."

"You, Mr. Masters, are a liar."

"Please. My friends call me Charlie."

She gave him a soft smile. "All right. Charlie…you're a liar." Even though she meant it as a joke, she could tell her words landed a blow by how his smile shrank a few inches.

"Well, I guess I've been called worse," he said with a sad, self-effacing humor.

At the odd flicker of emotions crossing his handsome

face, Gisella wished she could take her words back but before she got the chance, he walked away.

She followed, trying to keep her eyes averted from his broad shoulders, firm butt and muscled legs, but it was impossible.

No. No. No. No more bad boys.

He stopped briefly to retrieve his cane from the floor, but then continued on to the front door.

"I guess I'll see you around," Charlie said after crossing the threshold. He waited, giving her one more chance to talk about the kiss.

Instead, Gisella lowered her eyes and nodded.

"Goodbye." He turned and walked away.

Gisella slowly closed the door—and locked it.

Chapter 12

Charlie had no memory of driving back home. All he could do was replay the image of Gisella dancing in her living room in a lacy blue panties-and-bra set. No way would he ever forget it. Every detail from the heart-stopping curve of her breasts, the roundness of her full hips and even her long, shapely legs were now permanently branded in his mind.

He squirmed in the seat of his rental car, trying to give his erection a little more breathing room.

And what about that kiss?

He never dreamed she could taste that sweet. With very little effort he remembered how her silken tongue swept through his mouth and stole a part of his soul. It was just that erotic and sensual. No woman had ever kissed him like that.

Ever.

The only frustrating part was that it ended too soon.

One moment he was lost in heaven, and in the next all he saw was orange fur and sharp claws. But even the attack of the killer cat was worth that brief moment of intimacy. By the time he took a break from his long daydream, Charlie was back at his apartment and sprawled across his bed.

Seconds later, he was groaning and wishing the kiss had been longer or that he had reached out to feel the weight of her breasts in his hands. He did remember them being pressed against his chest and confirming that those babies were indeed real.

What he wouldn't give for the chance to see if her luscious mounds were just as beautiful as the rest of her. Charlie's breath thinned in his lungs as he closed his eyes and allowed the memory of strawberries to fill his senses.

Sighing, Charlie lost himself in the short memory and wondered why he'd never felt like this before. He ached just to be able to run his fingers through her hair or rain kisses along her collarbone.

For a woman who spent her life baking sugary treats, Gisella had a body any Hollywood celebrity would kill for. Small waist. Round hips. Flat stomach.

He wondered if her nipples were the color of brown sugar or maybe amber with a hint of gold. Charlie played with the images his head like it was a hologram in his mind. He gave it some serious consideration and finally decided her nipples would be the color of brown sugar and then went on to wonder about other intimate parts.

Brazilian wax?

Groomed?

Au naturel?

More important than that was, what did the other parts of her taste like? These were mysteries he was now obsessed with solving. And he *will* solve them.

Behind his closed eyelids, Gisella's saucy smile beamed, and her seductive walk entranced him. Now he pictured her crawling up his bed. Fantasy Gisella reached inside his pants with the promise to ease the ache of his throbbing erection.

Her hands were soft and smooth as silk, and their gentle stroking was torturously long and slow.

"Oh, God," he moaned, his toes curling against the bed. He wanted this woman, more than he'd ever wanted anyone. If fantasizing was the only way he could have her, then it would just have to do.

For now.

"*I know what you want,*" Fantasy Gisella whispered huskily in her erotic accent.

He didn't answer. He just watched as she positioned herself to straddle him and then eased down with all the grace of ballerina.

Tight.

Warm.

Wet.

As she began to ride, breathing became secondary to the intense emotions swirling inside of him. "Gisella… Gisella…"

It was all he *could* say and all that he *wanted* to say. He exploded like a rocket, every ounce of his energy zapped in an instant. But he was far from being satisfied.

It wasn't wise to pursue a new relationship. Not with all that he had on his plate. It was too late for that. He was closing chapters in his life, not starting new ones. It wouldn't be fair for him or her. Yet, he *had* to see her again. Even though reason and common sense told him to stay away, his heart and body had plans of their own.

Gisella opened her shop bright and early Monday morning. It was a new day, and she was determined to put yesterday's embarrassment to the back of her mind.

But it wasn't working—just like it hadn't worked yesterday.

There was a serious issue at play here. The craziness that she couldn't tell the difference between a fantasy and a real man standing in her living room was too disturbing.

Two of Gisella's part-time workers, Krista and Pamela, darted wary glances Gisella's way every time she'd slammed down a pot or dropped a tray of eggs. They had never seen her like this, and with all the mumbling Gisella kept doing they were too afraid to ask what was wrong.

After making one too many mistakes, Gisella snapped. "Okay! So you kissed him." She slammed her fist into a pile of flour and caused an atomic white mushroom cloud to cover her face.

Krista and Pamela crept toward the front of store in case their boss turned postal. Death by chocolate didn't sound so cute today.

Choking and waving the flour from her face, Gisella turned and marched to the large walk-in cooler to calm down. By the time Isabella breezed through a few hours later, Gisella had pulled herself together and was at least managing to get *some* of her recipes right.

Isabella reviewed a few spreadsheet issues with her, but by the time she left the shop, Gisella realized that she hadn't heard a single word the woman said.

Gisella sailed into the afternoon, edgy and distracted. Edgy because she thought everyone knew what she'd done and distracted because Charlie's phone number was burning a hole in her pocket. She was supposed to give the number to her sister last night when she called but she never quite got around to doing it. Not that she didn't have the opportunity, it's just that, well, she wasn't exactly comfortable with her sister calling her…what? Fantasy lover?

She did, however, casually bring up his name. This time she listened carefully to what her sister said as well as what she didn't say. Anna couldn't be baited; she just smoothly changed the subject.

What did that mean?

Were Charlie and her sister an item back in college? *That* thought was more troubling than the kiss. She dropped another pan, cursed a blue streak—both in French and in English.

Krista cleared her throat. "You have a visitor."

Gisella frowned. "Who is it?"

"I don't know." Krista shrugged. "Some guy," she said, her eyes sparkling. "Some incredibly handsome guy, if that helps."

Charlie. Gisella blinked stupidly up at her.

"Is everything all right?" Krista asked.

When she didn't readily respond, Krista asked, "Do you want me to get rid of him?"

"Uh, no." Gisella stood. "Just…tell him I'll be right up."

Frowning, Krista nodded and walked off.

Gisella quickly tried to dust the excess flour from her apron, but after surviving a large white funnel cloud, she gave up. Acknowledging that she was both excited and nervous, Gisella coached herself to stay cool. "You can do this." At least she hoped she could. This was like being a teenager all over again.

For an extra touch, she removed the hairnet and clip from her head and then strolled to the front of the shop with her heart in her throat.

But it wasn't Charlie waiting for her.

"Hello, Gisella."

"Robert?"

Chapter 13

"Sorry, Mr. Masters, but the Johannesburg contract has gone to McGraw-Hill Construction."

Charlie's heart sank as he gripped the phone receiver. "How is that possible? There wasn't supposed to be a decision until next month," he said, exasperated. "I've already booked my flight to South Africa."

"I'm sorry, but they announced their decision this morning," the nameless executive said emotionlessly.

Charlie plopped back in his chair, barely able to restrain his stream of curses. He didn't need this right now, but what else was there to say? No point in shooting the messenger.

After a couple of deep breaths, Charlie nodded against the phone. "Thank you for your time," he said gruffly and then dropped the hand unit back onto the cradle.

For a while, all he could do was sit in his chair and stare at the phone. What was he going to do? Disgusted when he couldn't think of a plan of action, he swiveled his chair and stared out of the window.

Charlie remembered the first time he'd looked out on the concrete and glass landscape. He felt like he was sitting on top of the world and there was nothing he couldn't accomplish.

Now…he felt lost.

Everything, it seemed, was falling apart, crumbling at his feet.

"Mr. Masters, you have a call on line one," Jackson announced over the speakerphone.

"Thank you." He turned around to the console and picked up the call. "Charles Masters."

"Charlie, I'm glad I've finally caught up with you."

Rolling his eyes, Charlie dropped his head against the palm of his hand. "Dr. Weiner, I've been meaning to call you."

The ensuing beat of silence hinted that the good doctor didn't exactly buy that line.

"I called to see if we can get you scheduled for that bone marrow test. It's important we get this done as soon as possible."

"Of course, um…I'll need to check my schedule…"

There was another awkward silence before Dr. Weiner said, "Look, Charlie. I know that this must really be hard for you. It's not uncommon when patients get this kind of news that to go into self protection mode. Denial. They think the longer they don't know something the better.

This isn't going to go away. In this case, it could be a fatal mistake. What you don't know *can* hurt you."

"I just…" Charlie stopped and drew a deep breath. "I just need some more time."

"You don't have much of that, Charlie."

But I feel fine!

"Look, I'm not going to lie to you. If your numbers are as severe as your blood work indicates, your chance for survival is extremely low. We have to get on top of this now."

After the doctor listened to Charlie's breathing for a few seconds, he added, "I'm going to have the nurses schedule you for the test at two o'clock on Friday at Northside, all right?"

Charlie nodded and then remembered that the doctor couldn't see him. "I'll be there," he lied.

"Good."

"Robert, what are you doing here?" Gisella asked with a sense of awe and suspicion.

International fashion model Robert Beauvais slid on his multimillion-dollar smile. "I came to see you," he said. He swept his arms open. "Now how about a kiss for your fiancé?"

From behind the sales counter, Krista and Pamela sighed.

Gisella crossed her arms. "You mean *ex*-fiancé, *n'est-ce pas*?"

"Semantics." He shrugged.

"We broke up over a year ago."

The reminder failed to erase his smile, and since she didn't rush dramatically into his arms, he took the initiative to close the gap between them in two strides. When his long muscled arms wrapped her into a smothering bear hug, Gisella thought she'd gag off his overpowering cologne.

"Ah, Gigi, you don't know how much I've missed you," he murmured against her ear.

Despite his handsome looks and his perfectly proportioned body, Gisella wasn't the least bit turned on. Pushing him back, she wiggled out of his grasp. "This is not the time or place," she warned.

He released her and then watched her to march back behind the counter.

"Gigi—"

"Stop calling me that!"

"But—"

Mercifully, Gisella was literally saved by the bell when two women entered the shop. "Hello, can I help you?" she asked, slapping on a bright smile.

A plus-size older woman with a sharp silver bob haircut smiled warmly. "Yes. I heard so much about your shop. I'd like to buy a dozen of your chocolate strawberry mousse truffles."

"Excellent choice!" Gisella exclaimed, a tad animated.

"Oh, I'll get them," Pamela volunteered.

"I'd like two dozen of the coconut clusters," the other woman added.

"I'm on it," Krista said.

Gisella could've chewed nails when she was once again stuck with having to deal with her ex.

"I missed you," Robert said, reaching for her hands.

She jerked them back across the counter and folded her arms across her chest.

"Paris is not the same without you," he continued undaunted.

"Robert…"

"Now," he said, holding up a hand. "I know I've made some mistakes, but I want you to know that I'm a changed man. I came here to apologize."

"You flew all the way here *just* to apologize?"

He nodded, but then added, "I also have a fashion shoot over at—"

"Figures."

"C'mon. Don't be like that." He cocked his head and leveled his best puppy-dog expression on her.

The shop's bell rang again, and this time the store experienced an afternoon rush.

However, Robert surprised her when he just stood back, content to wait. Forty-five minutes later, he pulled her aside again. "I mean it. I miss you. Come back to me."

Gisella stared, dumbstruck. Was he for real?

Confidence radiated in Robert's smile. *"J'ai t'aimé toujours."*

"If you loved me you wouldn't have cheated on me." She rolled her eyes and tried to walk away.

Robert grabbed her by the hand but she twirled around and snatched it back. "No, Robert. It's over. I've moved on." Too angry to notice the shop's sudden silence, Gisella moved forward and jabbed her finger into the center of his chest.

"You broke my heart," she hissed. "While I was off foolishly planning to spend the rest of my life with you, you were off sleeping with half of Europe."

Robert realized they were the center of attention and

smiled awkwardly. "Could you lower your voice? Everyone is watching us," he whispered.

Gisella shook her head. It was hard to believe that at one time she thought he hung the moon and stars. It wasn't until she left France and did some soul searching with the Lonely Hearts Club did she realize just how unhappy and unfulfilled she was in their relationship. She suffocated under Robert's ego and resented the fact that he never encouraged her to pursue her own dreams, even if it was just to run a small bakery.

Now, there she was standing before one of the handsomest men in the world and she felt…nothing. Absolutely nothing. "Go home, Robert," she said in the kindest voice she could manage.

"Gigi." He cocked his head. "It's me you're talking to. There's no need to play hard to get. I *know* you miss us being together."

"Robert—"

"Do you know how many women that would *love* to take your place?"

"As far as I'm concerned they're more than welcome to have you."

Disbelief rippled across Robert's face. A second later, it turned into suspicion. "Is there someone else?"

Mon Dieu!

"Is there?"

As if summoned by some magical power, the shop's door opened, and in walked Charlie.

Seizing the opportunity, Gisella practically flew to Charlie's side. "Ah, sweetheart, there you are!"

Frowning, Charlie glanced around. When he saw that there was no one behind him, he pressed a hand against his chest. "Who, me?"

Gisella laughed and wrapped her arm around his waist. "Stop being silly, darling. Of course I'm talking to you." She leaned up on her toes and pressed a butterfly kiss against his lips. Her performance was undoubtedly worthy of a Razzie Award for Worst Performance by a Non-Actress, but she smiled up at Charlie, praying desperately that he would play along.

The woman must have a split personality, Charlie thought. He looked from her to the tall brother that was glaring at them and put the pieces together. Easing on a wide smile, Charlie slid his arms around Gisella. "Well, I'm glad to see you're over that little lover's spat we had last night," he covered and then swooped down for a real kiss.

A deeper kiss.

A longer kiss.

Krista and Pamela sighed.

Gisella's pretense easily melted beneath the heat of such overwhelming passion. Her hold tightened around his waist when his tongue wickedly mated with her own. In no time at all her body overheated and the delicious sensations coursing through her left her trembling like a leaf.

Robert cleared his throat.

Charlie and Gisella kept kissing.

Robert tried again, this time sounding like he was trying to hack up a lung.

Charlie finally pulled away, mainly because Gisella lacked the strength.

"I take it that this is your new boyfriend," Robert droned sarcastically.

"What?" Gisella's eyes fluttered open. "Oh, yeah." She started to step back, but Charlie's arms locked into place. It was just as well since she doubted her legs would hold up on their own. "Um, Robert this is Charlie. Charlie, honey, this is Robert…my *former* fiancé."

"Former fiancé?" Charlie finally glanced at Robert.

"I'm sure she's mentioned me," Robert said confidently.

"No. Not really."

Robert's smile dropped.

Gisella forced back a laugh.

The men's keen gazes slowly assessed one another and, judging by their faces, neither was too impressed with the other.

"Well, I see you two are quite an item," Robert said and then clenched his jaw. "How long have you been dating?"

"Six months," Gisella answered the same time as Charlie replied "Two months." They glanced at each other and then switched positions.

"Two months."

"Six months."

Suspicion crept back into Robert's eyes. "I see."

An awkward silence drifted over the shop.

"I have to tell you," Charlie said. "I've never been happier since Gisella came into my life."

"Thanks…sweetheart." She laughed awkwardly. "I feel the same."

"I mean, the sex is like…incredible."

Gisella's eyes bulged.

A few women snickered and reminded Gisella that they had an audience. "Okay, *honey*. We don't need to talk about that."

"At first I didn't think I'd be able to keep up," Charlie added almost conspiratorially. "But my baby here was determined to coach me out of my shell. Ain't that right, *sweetie?*"

Instead of answering, she leaned forward and hissed, "I'm going to kill you."

"I love you, too, baby." He locked her chin between his fingers and silenced her with another kiss.

Forgotten once again, Robert coughed. "Well, that's that. I guess I should wish you two luck."

"Thanks, man. I appreciate that."

"Don't mention it." Robert's gaze drifted to Gisella. "It was nice seeing you again, Gigi. *Bon chance.*"

"*Au revoir,* Robert."

His smile gone, Robert turned and walked out.

Gisella sighed in relief.

"You know," Charlie said. "You come up with the damnedest reasons to kiss me when all you have to do is ask."

Chapter 14

"You're incorrigible," Gisella said. "I swear I would slap you if I wasn't so grateful for you helping me out of a sticky situation."

Charlie's brows cocked in amusement. "You're welcome."

The shop hummed with activity again. "The drama up here beats anything I've seen of *General Hospital* in the last ten years," one woman said, laughing.

"The men are better-looking, too," her friend added as they left the shop with their arms loaded down with cake boxes and store bags.

Charlie leaned forward and whispered in Gisella's ear. "Frankly, I thought the leading lady was pretty hot, too."

She rolled her eyes but couldn't stop a smile from carving onto her face. "What are you doing here anyway?"

Charlie decided to dance around the truth. "Well, I was out feeling sorry for myself and thought that maybe one of your delicious cakes would cheer me up. Had I known that you were giving out chocolate kisses all willy-nilly, I would've come by sooner…and more often."

He watched as her cheeks darken and he had another urge to kiss her. This time when he leaned forward, she leaned back.

"What are you doing?"

"What does it look like, sweetie?"

Belatedly, Gisella realized that she was still locked in his embrace. She cocked her head up at him with a sneaky suspicion that he was more than content to hold her. "You can let go now. The show is over."

"Are you sure, love muffin?" He pressed her closer. "Maybe we should keep the ruse up just in case he's outside watching us."

Gisella's gaze darted to the storefront window. Her eyes scanned the outside perimeter. Just when she was about to sigh in relief, her eyes caught sight of Robert sitting behind the wheel of a black Escalade across the street.

"*Mon Dieu.* He is out there."

"He is?" Charlie tried to turn to see for himself.

"Don't look." She pulled his body around, but only succeeded in placing her back against the glass and giving Charlie the street view.

"Ah, there he is," Charlie said, frowning. "What's the story with this guy? Is he a stalker or something?"

"No." Gisella shrugged. "I don't think he is, anyway."

"Maybe we should give him a good show." Charlie lowered his head but only to brush their noses together.

"What are you doing now?"

"You want to make it look good, don't you?"

She hesitated, but then forced herself to relax. "Why won't he just go away?"

"Maybe he's whipped," Charlie said, grinning. "You look like the kind woman that could whip a man without batting an eye. You probably do adorable things like dance around the house in sexy lingerie and then throw a killer pussy in a man's face."

She gasped.

"A pussycat…I meant a pussycat."

"Sure you did." She tried again to wiggle out of his arms only to have him tighten his hold.

"Wait. Wait. Wait. He's looking again."

Before she could verify, Charlie swooped low and kissed her. This one was even more intoxicating than the last. He didn't understand what was happening. He just couldn't get enough. When they broke apart, they were both out of breath and had to rest their foreheads together.

"Is he still watching?" Gisella asked, panting.

Charlie cast a quick sidelong glance. The Escalade was gone. "Yeah. He's still there."

"Maybe I should go out there and talk to him again. I can't imagine what made him think we could get back together."

"Maybe *I* should have a talk with him."

She chuckled.

"What? Even with a bad ankle I can take him."

"It's not that," she laughed.

"Then what?"

"I don't know. You just struck me as being a lover, not a fighter."

Charlie's cheeks dimpled as a sly smile hooked into place. "You picked up on that, did you?"

"Actually I think it was the warning about you being a low-down, lying, sex-crazed egomaniac that some vet needed to put out of his misery to save unsuspecting women from being nothing but notches on his bedpost."

Charlie's hold loosened. "Damn, woman. That's one hell of memory you got there."

"I only remember things worth remembering."

Completely charmed and fascinated, Charlie took a chance and said, "Go out with me."

"No," she answered simply.

"No?" he repeated. "You don't want to at least think about it?"

"Hmm…no."

"Damn. You really know how to hurt a man's feelings."

She reached behind her back and pried open his arms. "You're a big boy. You can handle it."

Even though her words were soft and her smile was kind, the rejection felt like a steel punch to the gut. "May I ask why?"

Gisella quirked up her brows. "Honestly?"

"Go for it."

"To go out with you would be no different than going out with Robert. Both of you aren't looking for anything serious. You view women as playthings and give very little thought to their feelings as you cast them aside when you're done with them."

Charlie's arm finally fell to his sides. "That's not true…entirely."

"Sorry if I hurt your feelings." She flashed him an apologetic smile. "I better get back to work."

Charlie wasn't ready to give up. "What if I said that I was a changed man?"

"I wouldn't believe you."

"You don't pull any punches, do you?"

"I believe in being honest."

"Oh. Is that right?" Charlie's face lit up. "Then maybe I should go outside and share a little honesty with pretty boy Robert about our so-called relationship?" He took one step toward the door.

"No!" Gisella grabbed him by the waist again.

"Ooh. I love it when you play rough." Charlie laughed at her panic-stricken face.

Pamela, Krista and a couple of new customers whipped their heads in Gisella's direction.

"Sorry," she said to the small crowd and then narrowed her gaze at Charlie.

"Sounds to me that someone is a bit of a hypocrite," he said.

"All right. You got me. Sometimes honesty is *not* the best policy."

"Go out with me."

"No."

"Then I have to talk to Robert." He faked another move toward the door.

Gisella's grip tightened. "That's blackmail."

He shrugged with a crooked grin. "Sometimes a man has to take desperate measures to avoid eating alone. Trust me. I'm not exactly proud of myself right now." He glanced out the window. "Oh. He's looking again." Charlie's lips attacked. This time he made up his mind to take his fill of her. As a result, there was a lot of moaning and pressing together.

"Damn. Get a room already," a male customer commented as he exited with his purchases.

At long last, Charlie pulled away while Gisella wobbled on her legs with her eyes still closed.

"Say you'll go out with me."

"I…"

"Tomorrow night," he pressed. "I promise I'll be on my best behavior. I'll take you to the best restaurant."

Her eyes fluttered open. "I…can't."

"You gotta eat. A woman can't live off chocolate alone."

"I…shouldn't."

Sensing victory, he smiled. "But you will."

Their eyes locked. Gisella nibbled on her bottom lip, contemplating. "Just dinner?"

"Just dinner," he promised.

After listening to both the devil and the angel on her shoulders, Gisella took a leap of faith. "All right. I'll go out with you."

Charlie tried to celebrate by stealing another kiss, but Gisella whipped her head and peered out the window. "Heeey. He's not out there." She whirled back toward Charlie. "How long has he been gone?"

"Ten, fifteen minutes." At her gasp, he delivered a quick peck on her nose and winked. "Pick you up tomorrow at seven-thirty."

Chapter 15

"What in the hell was I thinking?" Gisella asked herself for the umpteenth time. She stumbled into her sister's apartment with her arms weighed down with groceries. "There's no way I can go out with him. I'm supposed to stay away from his kind," she argued. "He's a womanizer. A dog."

In the kitchen, she plopped everything onto the counter and nearly slumped to the floor herself. "And on the other hand, the man sure can kiss." She sighed.

Sasha meowed and danced around Gisella's feet. "Don't worry. I haven't forgotten about you," she said, gathering up her energy and retrieving a can of cat food from the cabinet.

After setting down Sasha's food and water, Gisella headed toward the shower, debating whether she needed to make it a hot one or a cold one since her mind and body kept responding to the memory of Charlie's kisses.

She settled on hot. When she closed her eyes to enjoy the pulsing water against her skin, Charlie floated around in her head with his soft lips and talented tongue. It was as if he had made love to her mouth. That was the only way to describe it.

Where was her shame, standing in the middle of her shop, *in front of Robert,* and allowing Charlie to hold and seduce her like that? And why was it that she craved for him to do it again?

She sighed, remembering how each time his tongue dipped and caressed her own, her heart had skipped a beat, but that was nothing compared to how her body tingled whenever the tips of her breasts pressed against his chest.

"I don't know why you're fighting it," Fantasy Charlie whispered in her ear. *"You know you want me."*

That was an understatement.

Before her imagination got carried away, Gisella shut off the water and climbed out of the shower. She dried off and rushed through her regime of oils and lotions as an attempt to keep Fantasy Charlie at bay. To be more contrary, she dressed in her old two-piece cotton pajamas instead of anything lacy or satiny.

"I still think you look sexy," Fantasy Charlie said, stretching across the bed.

"Oh, go away," she said. She climbed into bed and gave him her back.

Fantasy Charlie chuckled.

Maybe she should cancel the date. What was the point

in going out with him? She still didn't know the story between him and her sister. The last thing she wanted was Anna's leftovers.

Plus, would she be able to handle herself and keep her knees locked against a man so charming and charismatic?

"You're kidding, right?" Fantasy Charlie rolled over and laid his head against her arm. He smiled. *"We both know how tomorrow night is going to end."*

Her heart raced at the thought of their different shades of brown skin rubbing against each other.

Fantasy Charlie winked.

She swallowed.

"You shouldn't have agreed to that date," the angel on her shoulder scolded.

"Hey, I'm a changed man," Fantasy Charlie protested.

Gisella glanced up into his dancing hazel eyes while doubt crept around in her mind.

The devil on her left shoulder laughed. "I say we jump his bones the minute he shows up at the door."

"I second that motion," Fantasy Charlie said.

"You stay out of this," Gisella snapped.

He held up his hands in surrender. *"All right. But maybe you should answer the phone."*

She frowned at him and in the next second, the phone rang. Gisella whipped her head toward the nightstand and then back toward Fantasy Charlie.

He was gone.

Hesitantly, she answered. "Hello."

"I'm dreaming about tomorrow night," the *real* Charlie informed her in a deep, sexy baritone. "What about you?"

Gisella hedged on how to answer.

"Hello?"

"Yeah, I'm here," she said.

"You're not thinking about canceling, are you?" he asked with a note of trepidation.

She shrugged. "What if I said yes?"

"I'd remind you that we made a deal. One date in exchange for my silence. Remember?"

"Yes, but—"

"I'd hate to have to drive over to the Ritz Carlton and knock on Robert's room to have a man-to-man talk."

Gisella frowned. "You know where he's staying?"

"Let's just say that I like to take out insurance when brokering important deals." He chuckled.

She groaned.

"And don't bother trying to make me feel guilty about blackmailing you," he added. "I've already prayed for forgiveness."

Finally laughing at the situation and his tactics, Gisella gave up. "All right. You win."

"Touchdown. Picture me dancing in the end zone."

His laugh was infectious. Gisella smiled, turned off the light on the nightstand and burrowed beneath the sheets. "How did you get this number?"

"The Internet, remember."

"You're a regular detective."

"I view it as going after something I want."

"Do you always get what you want?"

After a long silence, he answered, "Not always. No."

There was unmistakable note of sadness in his voice. Gisella wondered at its source, but hesitated in asking.

"Anyway," Charlie said, snapping out of his melancholy. "I called because I wanted to tell you to dress sexy-casual tomorrow night. The more leg the better, but if you want to tease me with some cleavage action, too, I won't complain."

She laughed at his audacity. "Thanks for the information."

"Don't mention it. Can you dance?"

"I can hold my own…as long as my partner isn't a stripper pole. I'll leave that fine art to some of the other women you date."

"Ooh. Frenchie has claws. No wonder you and Killer get along so well."

She giggled. "Sasha is not a killer."

"Yeah, right. That orange puffball is lucky there's no such thing as a kitty jail, or I would have had her butt hauled downtown."

Gisella warmed at the sound of his laughter and realized that it was something that she could easily get used to hearing.

"It's late," he said. "I better let you get some sleep."

She didn't want to hang up, but wouldn't allow herself to admit it.

"Sweet dreams, Gisella."

"Sweet dreams."

Charlie disconnected the call and then smiled up at the ceiling in his darkened bedroom. With everything that was going on in his life, he couldn't believe that he'd found something so precious. He couldn't believe how much he was looking forward to his date with Gisella. He already missed holding and kissing her.

I've picked a hell of time to fall in love.

He flinched and his smile evaporated. Why on earth had he used the L-word? Surely, he wasn't *in love*. He hardly knew the woman.

Sure she was beautiful and charming. And maybe there was something about the way she looked at him that in one minute he felt like an awkward teenager and in the next he felt dominant and masculine.

Charlie rolled onto his side and stared at the wall.

Maybe there was something about the way their bodies snapped together like pieces of a puzzle when he kissed her. It was as if they were a natural extension of each other. And whenever their mouths melded together, it was explosive.

No. He couldn't wait for tomorrow night.

"Remember, you promised to be on your best behavior," Fantasy Gisella said, suddenly appearing next to him.

"Trust me. I'm going to be the *perfect* gentleman."

The next day crawled at a snail's pace. Every five minutes, Charlie's gaze found its way to a watch or a clock. Once, he tried to tell the time by the angle of the sun. During meetings and conference calls, his mind kept drifting to the night's possibilities.

Charlie attempted a few more black book calls, but majority of the B's and C's had either changed or disconnected their numbers.

Taariq dropped by and invited him to the Jocks and

Jill's Sports Bar for lunch. He agreed but hardly paid attention to the food or the conversation.

"Are you all right, man?" Taariq asked. "I feel like I'm boring you or something."

Charlie blinked out of his trance and shook his head. "Sorry, bro. What were you saying?"

Taariq eyeballed him and then lowered his fork—an event that never happened when red meat was in the vicinity. "What's up with you? Me and the fellahs have been noticing you haven't exactly been acting like yourself."

"I don't know what you mean," Charlie lied.

"C'mon, man. What do I look like to you?"

Charlie almost laughed, especially since he was trying not to stare at the large bald spot Bobby had shaved on the side of his head.

"We're boys, remember?" Taariq said. "We've known each other for sixteen years. I know when something's up with you, man. Why don't you just spit it out?"

Guilt erupted in Charlie like a geyser. Here he was calling old flames and readily confessing the doctor's prognosis and he'd yet to tell the truth to the closest people around him. Mainly because once they knew, his life would irreversibly change. He wasn't ready for that right now.

"Nah, man. Everything's fine," he insisted, this time with his best poker face.

Their eyes locked for a long time before Taariq gave him a slow nod, but his eyes called him a liar.

Gisella tried on every dress in her closet—twice—and still didn't like any of them. Breaking sister rule number one, she went into Anna's room to raid her closet. It didn't help since 1. they had different body types, and 2. Anna's evening clothes were purchased back in the 1990s.

Sasha apparently found the whole thing amusing and followed Gisella from room to room.

In the end, Gisella decided on a short pale peach number that fell mid-thigh with a bubble hem. She felt self-conscious about her arms in the spaghetti straps, but confident that Charlie would be more than pleased about the amount of cleavage the dress displayed.

She accessed the various angles in the mirror about a hundred times and was just about to convince herself to change yet again, when the doorbell rang.

"He's early," she gasped. She turned toward Sasha curled up at the foot of the bed. "How do I look?"

Sasha cocked her head and then quickly dismissed Gisella to focus back on her own grooming needs.

"Thanks a lot." She took a final glance into the mirror and then rushed to answer the door. However, when she opened it her heart dropped.

"Nicole…Emmadonna…Jade…what are you girls doing here?"

The members of the Lonely Hearts Club shared their own astounded looks as their gazes raked over her.

Nicole jutted out a hip and crossed her arms. "We came to take you out," she said. "We figured with Anna still out of town that you'd want some company. Looks like we were wrong."

"Uh, er…"

Without waiting for an invitation, Nicole waltzed into the apartment. Her two cohorts followed.

Jade shook her head. "Here we are planning a girls night out, and you're creeping out the back door. Who's the hot date?"

Gisella's eyes bulged. No way was she telling this group she had a date with a man they considered to be the undisputed enemy to womankind. "Um, no one," she said, finding her tongue. The lie would have been more convincing if she wasn't standing in front of them in a three-hundred-dollar dress. "I have a business engagement."

"A *business* engagement," Nicole echoed. "What, did I just fall off the turnip truck this morning?"

Deciding to come clean, Gisella tossed up her hands. "All right. I have a date, and he's going to be here any moment."

Emmadonna chuckled. "Is that French for 'get lost'?"

"Must be." Jade laughed.

Gisella felt desperate. "Ladies, please. Thank you so much for thinking about me. Maybe we can do it another time."

The women stared.

"Promise?" Gisella added.

"All right." Jade said and straightened her shoulders. "We'll leave…but let me use your bathroom first." She turned and marched toward the hallway.

"I'm after you," Emmadonna chimed.

Gisella panicked. They were stalling. "Ladies, ladies, please." She raced behind them.

"Ooh," Nicole smirked. "This must be serious. You really don't want us to know who this guy is."

Emmadonna planted a fist against her plush hips. "What's the matter? Is he ugly?"

"No," Gisella protested.

"Fat?" Jade suggested.

Emmadonna looked heated. "What, you got something against plus-size people?"

"No. I. Don't." Gisella was close to losing her patience. "Now will you please…?"

Jade stepped into the bathroom and closed the door.

Gisella tossed up her hands and swore in French.

Emmadonna's neck swiveled around. "Girl, you're acting like you're scared we're going to try and steal your man or something."

"Yeah. Calm down," Nicole said. "We're just going to check him out for you. Make sure his ass is on the up and up. What you got to drink up in here?" She headed toward the kitchen.

The doorbell rang.

Gisella froze.

"Ooh. That's must be him now," Nicole whooped. "I'll get it."

"No. Nicole, wait." Gisella rushed behind her, but Nicole had amazing speed for a woman in heels. Toward the end, the race seemed to move in slow motion.

Nicole's hand landed on the doorknob, Emmadonna and Jade cackled in the background, and Gisella screamed, "No," because she, alone, knew what was about to happen.

"Come on in, lover boy," Nicole sang, opening the door.

All playfulness died when Charlie stood smiling in the doorway.

He looked good. Damn good in a pair of white slacks and a pale green top. In his hand, he held a single long-stemmed rose. Definitely casual-sexy.

"Good evening," he said.

"Hi," Gisella greeted breathlessly behind Nicole.

The ever busy busybody whipped around and stabbed Gisella with an accusing glare before swinging it back to Charlie.

"Oh. Hell. Naw," Nicole shouted and then promptly slammed the door in Charlie's face.

Chapter 16

What just happened?

Charlie blinked at the closed door and hit instant replay in his head, but it didn't help. However, he could hear angry voices on the other side. He leaned forward and pressed his ear against the door. A mistake, given how his name seemed interchangeable with *dog, jerk, asshole* and a few other words that weren't fit for Christian ears.

Clearly, Gisella's friends weren't exactly fans of his.

When he'd heard enough, he straightened up and knocked on the door with his cane's handle. To be safe, he braced for anything.

Thankfully, Gisella answered the door, but he noticed her smile was strained. One glance at the three glaring witches was a sufficient explanation. "Ladies." He tilted his head in a half bow. "Problem?"

"You damn right there's a problem," snapped the obvious leader. "You've lost your rabbit-assed mind if you think we're about to let you take our girl out tonight."

Gisella's whipped her head around. "Nicole!"

"Gisella, girl. This man—"

"Enough!"

Charlie frowned. "Nicole, Nicole…" He searched through his mental Rolodex. A few images popped but none that resembled…"Wait a minute." He snapped his fingers and then entered the apartment. "I know you."

Nicole crossed her arms and cocked her head.

"Yeah. I remember now. You're Anna's friend from college." His lips quirked up. "The one that used to always pass out drunk at all the fraternity parties."

Nicole's face darkened. "Not always."

The friend to her right grabbed her by the arm. "Let's just go, Nic."

Charlie turned his attention to the attractive plus-size woman. "I know you, too, don't I?" He waited for his recollection to kick in.

"You sure do," the third woman said, with an unbelievable high-pitched voice. "You two hooked up at a club—"

"Jade, hush!"

"What, Em? You said—"

"That's it." Charlie snapped his fingers. "You tried to rape me at a bar once when I asked what you were drinking. Said something about dogs and bones and then jumped me."

"Emmadonna!" Her friends gasped.

Gisella snickered.

"*You* said that he was the one that—"

"I never said no such thing. Now let's go." Emmadonna clenched her purse strap, threw up her chin and then marched out of the apartment.

"But, Em," Jade said, rushing after her.

Nicole was the last to take her leave, but when she reached Gisella by the door, she cast a final glare at her. "Just wait until I talk to your sister."

"I make my own decisions, Nicole," Gisella said.

"Humph. We'll see." Nicole looked over her shoulder at Charlie. "As for you, try to keep it in your pants tonight." At last, she left the apartment.

Gisella closed the door behind her.

"Interesting group of friends you got there."

"Actually, they are my sister's friends." She drew in a deep breath. "I'm sorry about that."

"Don't be." He walked over to her, his limp less noticeable. "I'm the bad boy with the bad reputation. One that I unfortunately earned."

She gazed at him. "I have a long list of reasons why I shouldn't go out with you tonight. Your reputation being number one."

"I thought it was because I was blackmailing you," he said, smiling.

"That's number two."

He took a deep breath, fearing what she might say next.

"Like I was saying," she continued. "I have a long list of reasons *not* to go out with you and only one for why I should."

"And that is?"

Her beautiful, plump lips widened. "Because I *want* to."

"Sounds like a good reason to me." Charlie handed her the rose.

"Thank you." Gisella placed the delicate petals against her nose and inhaled its light fragrance.

To his surprise she stepped forward, leaned up on her toes and brushed a kiss against his cheek.

Charlie's eyes lit up. "Wow. What would I have gotten if I brought you a dozen?"

"I don't know." She shrugged. "Next time, bring a dozen and we'll find out."

He loved the way her eyes glinted when she flirted. Of course, he had to restrain himself from grabbing her and ravishing her on the spot. "Next time, eh?"

Gisella rolled her eyes.

"By the way, you look beautiful this evening."

"*Merci.* You look rather handsome yourself—but I think you know that."

Charlie winked. "Are you ready to go?"

"Let me just grab my purse and the wrap that goes with this. I'll be just a minute," she said.

"I'll wait right here."

Gisella left the living room just as Sasha made her grand entrance. Man and animal eyeballed each other, neither one trusting the other. The orange cat marched back and forth like an armed security guard parceling out meow warnings.

"I'm ready," Gisella said, returning and catching the ending of their tense stare down. "You two play nice." She laughed.

"I'm cool if she's cool." He opened the door.

"Mind if I ask where we're going?"

"Actually, I want it to be a surprise."

And a nice surprise it was, Gisella thought as they were escorted through the elegant Prime restaurant. The soft lighting and the contemporary elegance of the place made Gisella feel as if she was joining the city's posh elite.

"Would you like a bottle of wine?" their server asked.

"The house wine will be fine," Charlie said.

Gisella continued to look around, her face glowed when she stared out at the city's twinkling skyline.

"Do you like the restaurant?" he asked, watching her.

"It's lovely." She smiled. "I wasn't expecting grand. You said casual."

"This is casual, but if you want we can rush out of here and catch Arby's before it closes."

She laughed. "Maybe next time."

"Again with the next time." He leaned forward in his seat. "I'm beginning to suspect you like me."

"Maybe…or maybe I just like to play dress up every once in a while."

"Nice play." He wagged his finger. "You don't want me to get a big head."

"Don't you mean a *bigger* head?"

Charlie drew a deep breath and settled back in his chair. "You know, I think I'm heavily misunderstood."

Her delicate brows stretched. "Do you?"

"Absolutely," he said, putting on a serious face. "Women see a man like me, and they transfer their own perceptions of what I'm all about onto me. I very rarely have a say on the matter."

Gisella shook her head, smiling. "You said earlier that you earned your bad reputation. Which is it?"

He shifted in his chair. His Cheshire smirk wobbled into place. "I guess it would depend on one's definition of bad."

"Oh, really?"

"The definition varies between the sexes. For men, bad could be a good thing. Just as too much of a good thing could be bad. I like to think women believe I'm too much of a good thing. Anyway, I have a whole charting system on this if you ever want to come back to my place to study up on it."

Gisella's laughter was like music to his ears.

"Does that line usually work?" she asked.

"What line?" he asked innocently.

Their server returned and presented a bottle of the house wine. Charlie nodded and waited as the cork was popped and their glasses were filled before returning to their conversation.

"So tell me about Sinful Chocolate. It looks like you have quite a lucrative business going."

Gisella took a sip of her wine and wondered where to begin. "It looks that way. I'm really happy how it's all working out. I can't remember a time when I wasn't cooking or baking. In my family it's an expression of life…love…everything. When you cook for people there's a connection. For some it's even an art form. Just like music or a painting, it can create and elicit memories. Let's face it, no one is sad when they are eating a good meal."

Charlie looked at her as if she was an angel descended

from heaven. "If you cook half as good as you kiss I'm going to have to start calling you Mrs. Masters before long."

"If it's a princess-cut ring you just might have yourself a deal."

Charlie chuckled and then slowly realized that he hadn't stopped smiling since their date began. He adored how she had the tendency to talk with her hands or how her accent muddled some words and made others sound incredibly sexy. When their server returned, she allowed him to order for her and then when the food arrived, he was turned on by the many sounds she made when eating.

He hardly tasted his food. He was so enamored with everything about her he wasn't interested in anything else. Where had she been all his life, and how cruel was it for her to show up now?

"Charlie?"

Charlie reluctantly pulled his gaze away from Gisella to see an attractive woman head their way. He knew her. He was fairly certain.

She stopped at the table.

Joan? Lynn? Mya? No. That was that Girlfriends *show*.

"It's Lexi," she supplied. "When are you going to learn that TV name game doesn't work?"

Actually, she would be surprised, he thought.

"And who is your beautiful friend here?" Lexi asked.

Charlie shifted in his chair. A person would have to be deaf, dumb and/or stupid not to pick up on Lexi's thinly veiled jealousy.

"This is Gisella," he answered. "Gisella, meet Lexi."

"*Bonjour.*"

"Ah, French," Lexi cooed. "You're reeling them in from across the water now. Good for you. I think it's just so generous of you to *spread* the love."

Charlie's smile tightened. "Well, it was good seeing you again, Lexi."

Her fake smile dropped at the dismissal. "Fine. I'll see you around." She glanced at Gisella with a calculating sneer. "Have a…fun evening. It's likely all you're going to get."

Charlie and Gisella watched her leave.

Charlie relaxed.

Gisella asked, "Old girlfriend?"

"Something like that." Charlie grabbed his wineglass and drained it dry in one gulp.

"Humph." Gisella shook her head. "Bad boys and their forgotten toys."

Charlie didn't respond and hoped the subject would just drop.

Their dinner plates were removed, and dessert arrived with much fanfare, but it paled compared to Gisella's new orgasmic moans.

"You're killing me," he said playfully, hoping to reclaim their earlier mood.

"Oh, I'm sorry," she said, teasingly or innocently. He couldn't tell which.

"There's just so much moaning I can take," he warned. They lapsed back into their easy conversation, neither noticing how the restaurant was emptying.

"I have to ask you a question," she said after fidgeting for a while.

"Okay. Shoot."

She hesitated. Bit her lower lip.

"Must be serious," Charlie commented.

"What's the story between you and my sister?"

"Oh, that." Charlie stopped smiling.

"Where you two an item?"

"No." That part of the story was the easy part. "I misinterpreted her feelings toward me back in the day."

"Sounds like a habit of yours."

He blinked at the casual observance. "You might be right," he admitted.

"Tell me the story."

He did just that. From how they met to the ugly fight where Anna accused him of using her.

"To this day she was my only real female friend that didn't involve…you know."

Gisella nodded and looked much relieved.

"What did she tell you?" he asked.

"I haven't talked to her about it." She glanced up sheepishly. "I haven't *exactly* delivered your message yet. Sorry."

"Not *exactly* dependable, are you?" His smile returned.

"I was just afraid that you two…and I…forget about it."

"No, no, no. This sounds interesting." He leaned closer. "What were you afraid of?"

"Nothing. Forget I said anything."

"All right. But I'll get the truth out of you someday—somehow."

"There's just one thing I don't get," Gisella said. "Why did you look her up now? I mean, this happened so long ago."

Charlie dropped his gaze, his smile gone.

Gisella waited through the silence, sensing that wave of sadness again.

"No reason," he finally said. "She just crossed my mind again. Who knows, maybe you reminded me of her."

She couldn't prove it, but she thought he was lying to her.

Charlie glanced around. "It looks like we're the last ones here." He looked over at her empty plate. "Are you ready to go?"

She wasn't, but he clearly was. "Sure."

Gisella excused herself to the ladies' room while Charlie took care of the bill. At the vanity, she washed up and re-touched her makeup. The entire time, she wondered if she'd said something wrong. When she returned to their table, he was back to being his old charming self.

Maybe she'd imagined the whole thing.

It was past one a.m. when they returned to her apartment building. Gisella's nerves were so frayed over the thought of a good-night kiss that it felt as if the Cirque du Soleil troupe was performing in the pit of her stomach.

Should she invite him in? What would happen if she did?

"You know what will happen," the devil said, popping up on her shoulder.

"Well, I guess this is it," Charlie said, stopping in front of her door.

"Yeah. I guess so." She smiled through an awkward pause and then unlocked and opened her apartment door. "I, um, had a great time."

"So did I," he said, picking up on her nervousness. Usually, about now, Charlie would calculate and strategize on how to get invited in for a nightcap. But for some reason he didn't want to rush things with Gisella. This time, he wanted to do everything right. "Good night." He leaned forward and swept his lips against hers.

The electric jolt was instant and, as expected, their bodies snapped together completing the perfect puzzle. In truth, he could've held her all night and overdosed on the sweetness of her lips. He wanted her to know how special she was to him and in order to do that, he *couldn't* sleep with her.

He frowned at his conclusion. Had the day finally arrived Charlie Masters was *not* going to have sex with a beautiful woman?

Gisella was ready to throw caution in the wind and invite Charlie in for a nightcap and for anything else he wanted. She knew there was very good chance that she would regret her decision in the morning, especially if she woke to just a note on a pillow. There was little doubt this scene was routine for him, but there was also no denying just how much she wanted him. Maybe it would be worth the risk—as long as she reminded herself not to fall in love.

Then again, maybe it was a little too late for that, too.

When the kiss ended and the invitation was on the tip of her tongue, Charlie smiled and murmured a final, "Good night, Gisella. Sweet dreams." With that he turned and walked away, leaving Gisella standing in the hallway with her mouth open.

Chapter 17

One month later

"Y̲ou *still* haven't slept with him?" Waqueisha thundered before tossing her head back with a roar of laughter. "What did he do, turn in his playa's card?"

"Waqueisha," Isabella hissed. "You're not helping."

Gisella whisked a bowl of ingredients like she had a vendetta against eggs and flour. "We've been going out for a full month. A *month!* And all he does is drops me off at the door with a kiss good-night."

"Well, how are the kisses?" Isabella inquired gently.

"Wonderful…fantastic!" Gisella slammed the bowl on the counter. "Kissing isn't the problem. Getting him into my bed is. Hell, last night I was tempted to strip in the hallway just to get his attention. I mean, where is this sex-crazed egomaniac I keep hearing about? And why won't he have sex with me?"

"Don't forget the low-down, lying dog that needed to be put out of his misery part," Waqueisha reminded her. When the women glared at her, she turned defensive. "I'm just saying."

Gisella tossed her hands. "You know what? I don't even want to talk about it anymore. In fact, I'm not even sure I'm going to see him again."

"Sounds like somebody's in heat."

Isabella jabbed her hands on her hips. "Waqueisha, you're not helping."

"What? I'm just saying that your girl wants to get laid, and this Charlie dude needs to catch a clue."

Isabella started to argue when Gisella cut in, "She's right. I'm ashamed to say it, but I'm horny as hell, and Charlie is as cool as a cucumber."

"Have you thought about taking him to a seafood bar and feeding him oysters all night? They're supposed to be like some kind of aphrodisiac."

"I thought of that," Gisella said. "He's allergic to shellfish."

"Ms. Jacobs, there's a delivery for you," Krista said, poking her head back in the kitchen.

"Coming." Gisella sighed and washed her hands in the sink before rushing up front.

"Are you Ms. Gisella Jacobs?"

"Yes, sir," Gisella said, walking toward the UPS man.

"Sign here."

She quickly raced over and signed the package. "Amélie DeLorme. It's from *ma grandmère,*" she said, stunned and walked to the back office. What on earth was her grandmother sending her?

Sitting down at her small desk in her matchbox-sized office, Gisella ripped into the package. Buried beneath a mountain of packing popcorn was a large decorative wooden box.

"*Recettes secrètes.*" Gisella gasped. Her *grandmère*'s secret recipes. Barely able to contain her excitement, Gisella bounced in her chair and then carefully pulled open the top. Immediately, she recognized the beautiful pen strokes on the three-by-five decorative postcards. "I can't believe it."

Gisella glanced back at the UPS box and wondered if there was also a note. She searched through the packing peanuts and withdrew a lavender-colored envelope with her name written in the same elegant penmanship.

Grabbing the letter opener from her desk, she ripped the top and unfolded the delicate lavender stationery.

"Is it something good?" Isabella asked. She and Waqueisha popped their heads into in the office.

"It's more than good," Gisella sighed. "She sent me the recipe for *Amour Chocolat!*"

The announcement left Isabella and Waqueisha clueless.

"This means my little problem with Charlie Masters is over."

"You need to file bankruptcy?" Taariq braided his large hands and leaned over his desk. "Brother, I didn't even know you were in trouble. Why didn't you come to me sooner?"

Charlie drew in a deep breath and worried whether his massive migraine was going to do him in. "Nobody knew. I haven't told anyone. The last couple of years, I've done everything I could to stay afloat, but I'm going to have to shut down the office soon. I won't be able to make payroll past next week.

"This market has just dried up in Atlanta. There are too many commercial contractors like myself playing cutthroat politics for the few contracts that come available. Hell, I've even lost the bid on a few government and foreign contracts. Man, it's just time to just cut my losses and move on."

He looked over at his friend and appreciated the absence of sympathy and pity in his expression. "Can you help me out?"

"Sure." Taariq shrugged. "I just thought that you had your own set of corporate lawyers for this kind of thing."

"If I can't make payroll I certainly can't bankroll a team of expensive lawyers."

"I'm not exactly cheap, either," Taariq reminded him. A playful smirk hooked the corners of his lips. "But I guess I can see about getting you a discount, being that you're like family and all."

A genuine smile bloomed across Charlie's face. "Thanks, man. I appreciate that." He placed his fingers against his temples and gave them a vigorous rub.

"Are you all right, man?"

"Yeah. Sure. I've just been suffering from some killer migraines lately." Charlie flashed him a weak smile. "Probably from all this stress from the job."

"With Masters Holdings folding, how are you doing—financially, I mean? Is there anything I can help you with?"

"Nah, man. Thanks. Most of my personal situation is separated from the company. I still might have to give up a few toys until I launch into a second career, but other than that, I'm doing good. Thanks for asking."

Taariq nodded.

"Well, I better go. I'll get the financials together from the accounting department to you by the end of the week."

"Trust me. It's going to take you longer than a week to get everything we need together. But don't worry, if you need for me to roll up my sleeves to help out, you got it."

"Thanks, man. I appreciate it."

"Appreciate hell. You see about getting me an invitation to Momma Arlene's meals, and we can just about call this transaction square."

Charlie laughed. "Consider it done."

The men shook on it.

However, when Charlie stood to leave, he experienced a severe case of vertigo and wobbled on his feet before plopping back down.

"Whoa." Taariq leapt from his chair and raced around his desk. "What's going on with you?"

"I'm cool. I'm cool." Charlie shook his head. "Any way I can get some aspirin?"

"Sure. Hold on." Taariq quickly buzzed his assistant.

Less than a minute later, Charlie was handed two pills and a large glass of water. The whole time he could feel the weight of Taariq's gaze.

"Have you seen a doctor? You don't look so good."

Charlie chuckled and tried to dismiss his concerns. "It's just a migraine. Nothing serious."

"You've been having a lot of those lately."

"I already have one mother."

Taariq's hands shot up in surrender. "Hey, don't shoot the messenger."

"Don't worry, man. As soon as these pills kick in, I'll be good as new."

She didn't know what she was looking for. It was the second time she'd managed to gain access to the exclusive high-rise apartment and broke in to Charlie's bachelor pad. It was easy to do since her brother was head of security.

The last time she was in here, she'd totally trashed the place. But that, just like when she vandalized his car, she'd hoped the act of revenge would make her feel better.

It didn't.

Especially now that it seemed like the philandering playa had a new girlfriend.

French bitch.

In the last month, she'd followed them all over town. Every other night it seemed they were either going to some play or movie or concert or eating at the most exclusive restaurants. At first she thought she was mistaken about their relationship. As far as she could tell, Charlie and his foreign-exchange girlfriend had yet to spend the night together. It made no sense because just watching him with her, she could tell he was crazy about her.

Always smiling.

Always touching.

Always kissing.

The constant public show of affection was enough to make her gag. There's no doubt about it, Charlie Masters was in love.

So why weren't they sleeping together?

Was that the secret to winning his heart—keeping your legs closed? What kind of prehistoric thinking was that?

She drew a deep breath as her anger returned in full force. Her friends told her to stay away from him. Why didn't she listen?

She took another glance around the apartment, looking for something—anything—she could use to extract her next wave of revenge. But as soon as she walked into his bedroom, she was caught up in his world.

In his closet, she roamed her hands over his suits and shirts. At his chest of drawers, she sniffed his cologne and even dabbed a little bit on her wrists. The pinnacle, of course, was when she climbed into his bed and hugged his pillows against her chest.

Lost in her own fantasy, she almost didn't hear when the apartment's front door opened and then slam shut.

He's home.

She jumped off the bed and scrambled around in a circle, trying to think. Soon his heavy footsteps filled the hall.

I'm going to get caught.

She had seconds to find a hiding place.

After a hard day, Charlie entered his bedroom and started peeling out of his suit. He was looking forward to his date with Gisella. Just being around her was like a soothing balm to his soul. She calmed him. Grounded him.

She was everything a man could hope for—beautiful, funny and smart. As much as he wanted to make love to her, he was proud of himself for holding back. Without sex, he was free to discover Gisella the woman. He might not have appreciated her if he'd, like he usually did, rushed to sex.

Tonight, she said she wanted to cook him a homemade meal. She bragged that she could go toe-to-toe with his mother. If she could, he just might have to go through on his promise and buy her a ring.

He was leaning toward buying her one anyway.

Of course, he didn't know how she would feel about marrying a man who was on the verge of losing everything and whose days were possibly numbered.

Charlie ignored the pinprick of guilt for not keeping his doctor's appointments and for even ducking the bone marrow test. The main reason he'd bypassed the test was because he felt fine. How could he be dying when he felt as healthy as a horse?

Most of the time.

He thought about the increasing number of migraines he'd had, but he wasn't convinced that they weren't products of the amount of stress he'd been under on the job. Then there was the vertigo.

"I'm fine," he insisted with a firm shake of his head. He refused to think about the matter anymore. He needed to rush. There was just enough time for a quick shower before his date.

Charlie turned toward the adjoining bathroom and

stopped cold. His hackles rose unexpectedly and he cast a curious glance around the room. Something was wrong. Something wasn't quite right about the room.

His gaze skittered over toward the bed and he noticed the sheets were wrinkled. Didn't the maid come this morning? Just then he sniffed the air, but he only smelled his cologne.

"Okay, old boy. You're imagining things." He laughed and left the bedroom.

Underneath the bed, she watched Charlie disappear into the bathroom. She held her breath until he turned on the shower. Relieved, she dropped her head against the carpet and waited for her heartbeat to return to normal.

Soon after, Charlie started singing a lame version of New Edition's "Candy Girl," and she crawled out from her hiding place. Despite knowing that she needed to get the hell out of there, she instead crept toward the bathroom with the overwhelming desire to see Charlie naked.

You're going to get caught!

It was a real possibility, she knew. When she was just a few inches from the door, she stopped and stood there a full minute, debating.

Finally, she backed away and rushed to leave his bedroom. But at the door, she stopped again. Something caught her eyes.

A book.

She picked it up and flipped through its page. "Well, I'll be damned." A broad smile stretched across her face. She had just hit the jackpot.

* * *

Still singing, Charlie shut off the water and grabbed a towel. He walked back into his bedroom, patting himself dry when he heard the unmistakable sound of his front door slamming shut.

Chapter 18

It had been so long since Gisella had tried to seduce a man that she worried whether she even remembered how. Luckily, she had a secret weapon. Once she'd received her grandmother's recipe box, she immediately left the shop in search of the foreign ingredients for *Amour Chocolat*. Of course, once she told the women at the shop the urban legend surrounding the recipe they'd all clamored for a piece of the action.

"A date-rape cake," Fantasy Charlie said. He shook his head. *"It's a sad day in Gotham."*

"Stop it." Gisella frowned, carefully setting the night's dessert down on the kitchen counter. "It's not a date-rape cake…it's date-*enhancer* cake," she corrected.

"You say tomato."

"Desperate times call for desperate measures," she said.

"I'm starting to think that you're getting sick of me."

"No offense. But I'm ready for the real thing." She smiled and winked.

Like a tornado, Gisella hit the kitchen and prepared her favorite roasted herb chicken, steamed some vegetables and made sure that she had plenty of red wine. Since it was her first time cooking a home-cooked meal for Charlie, she wanted everything to be perfect.

After a record-breaking shower, a rush through some hot curlers and tossing on a simple black dress, the doorbell rang.

"Showtime." Fantasy Charlie's voice floated around in her head.

Sasha meowed from the corner of the bed.

"Wish me luck, girl." Gisella raced to the door. "Good evening."

Charlie, holding yet another single red rose, took his time allowing his gaze to roam over her body. "As usual, you look lovely," he praised.

"And you look equally debonair," she returned, accepting the rose. Gisella inhaled its fragrance and then turned to add it to the near two dozen, in different stages of bloom, sitting in a vase in the entryway.

"It smells wonderful in here," Charlie said.

"I hope you brought a hearty appetite." She closed the door behind him. "I plan on giving your taste buds a night they'll never forget."

"Be still my heart. You're talking the language of love now." Without warning, his arms snaked around her waist and pulled her pliant body toward him.

When he pressed his pillow-soft lips against hers, Gisella emitted a submissive whimper. She loved how easily he dominated her body or how with a flick of his tongue she was reduced to putty in his hands.

"I missed you," he panted when he pulled away.

"It hasn't even been twenty-four hours since our last date," she said breathlessly.

"It still felt like a lifetime."

Gisella knew exactly what he meant. Her body seemed to count the seconds from their last touch. "Did you remember the movie?"

He held up a video box. "Your favorite. *Mahogany*."

"Good boy. I just might keep you around."

Smiling into each other's eyes, they held each other a little while longer and swayed to the music inside their heads. In what was becoming the norm, Charlie pulled away when the outline of his erection pressed against her belly. She didn't understand why he continued to resist his attraction toward her.

"Now let's see if you can back up all that trash talk about being able to beat my momma's cooking."

"Oh, I can back it up. I just hope you brought my ring."

Charlie laughed as she led him by the hand toward the dining room. "Can I help you with anything?"

"You can light the candles and pour the wine," she said before heading off toward the kitchen.

Minutes later, Gisella set their dinner plates on the table. "*Bon appetit.*"

Charlie closed his eyes and dramatically inhaled the food's rich aroma. "Damn, woman. You already have my mouth watering." Before digging in, Charlie stood and pulled back her chair.

"Ah, a true gentleman." She sat down.

"I gotta take care of the cook." He brushed a kiss against her cheek and then returned to his seat. "I really appreciate you wanting to cook for me."

"It was my pleasure, and I fully expect for you to return the favor in the near future."

He laughed. "I don't know my way around the kitchen too much, but I can work a mean grill."

"Then barbeque it is."

Charlie took her hand and recited the Lord's prayer. Afterward, he clapped his hands and rubbed them together. Ready to dig in.

Anxious, Gisella watched. She wouldn't admit in a million years that she was actually nervous for his critique. As if sensing her anxiety, Charlie took his time cutting, inspecting and even smelling it again.

Gisella finally smacked him on the hand. "Stop it. You're killing me."

Laughing, Charlie took his first bite. Instantly, his eyes closed while he released a long moan of pleasure.

Gisella smiled as her chest puffed with pride.

"Oh, woman. You put your foot in this," he praised.

The smile melted off her face. "I did not!"

Charlie's eyes sprang opened before he rocked back in his chair laughing. "That's a Southern saying. It just means you put your best foot forward. You know. You gave it all you got."

"Oh." She fluttered a hand across her chest in great relief.

Charlie cut bigger and bigger pieces of his chicken and

then moaned louder and louder. The biggest compliment came when he blinked his big hazel eyes at her and asked for seconds. "I have to be honest. I didn't think you had it in you, but I'm going to have to give it to you. You can give Momma a run for her money."

"Thank you," she beamed, handing him his second plate.

"I just need to know whether you want a church or an outdoor wedding."

"I don't know. I'll have to get back to you on that." They laughed and then fell into easy conversation. Gisella imagined them doing this for years to come. She could picture them gray-haired with a loving family surrounding them. In that moment, she was the happiest woman on earth.

"You make sure you save room for dessert," she said. "I made something special just for tonight."

"Bring it on."

Gisella disappeared into the kitchen and then returned with the cake. Lifting the glass lid, she presented the intricate design of flowers and ribbons. *"Paraît bon?"*

"Looks beautiful." Charlie patted his stomach. "I'm going to have to double up my time in the gym being with you."

"There's other ways of working off extra calories," she said teasingly.

Charlie caught her meaning. "Is that right?"

She shrugged and then sliced him a piece of cake.

"Now what do we call this?" he asked accepting his dessert.

"It's a special recipe from my *grandmère*. It's called *Amour Chocolat*."

"'Love chocolate'?"

"More like 'chocolate love'."

Charlie's brows sprang up. "Sounds erotic."

"It is. Wait until you taste it."

"All right." Charlie dug in and his face immediately collapsed with pleasure. "Oh, this is gooooood," he moaned, and then stuffed another piece into his mouth. When he cleaned his plate, he turned to her. "I mean it. You have to marry me. Say you'll marry me."

"Stop it before I think you're being serious."

"I am serious."

It was hard to tell whether he meant it or whether it was the food talking. However, Gisella started to panic when he then sliced himself another piece of cake…a larger piece.

Was it possible to have too much? Could a person overdose on passion?

"Are you not going to have some?" he asked.

Gisella blinked out of stupor and sliced herself a thin piece. But one bite also had her moaning and shoveling it in.

"Wow." Charlie pulled on his collar. "Is it me, or is it getting hot in here?"

"It *is* a little warm." She checked the thermostat, but it read a cool seventy-four degrees.

"Everything looks normal," she said, returning to the living room. Gisella arms started tingling and then the sensation raced across her body. Suddenly she was very aware of her lacy bra brushing against her nipples as she walked.

Charlie watched her intently as she came back into the living room. She still had the sexiest walk he'd ever seen.

Those legs.

That butt.

Those hips.

Those breasts.

That face.

Charlie shifted in his chair, trying to give his erection a little more room. "That dress…you sure look good." He licked his lips.

Gisella watched the intriguing path of his tongue and stared fascinated at how it left his lips glistening beneath the candlelight. "Oh, goodness."

Charlie smiled and suggested, "Maybe we should go watch that movie now." The glint in his eyes said that the movie was the last thing on his mind.

"All right," she said, feverishly.

Charlie stood and carried their two wineglasses.

In the living room, Gisella turned on the ceiling fan, hoping the breeze would cool her down. She walked over to the DVD player, fumbled with the buttons before she realized she didn't have the movie. "Whew. Where's my head?" She turned around but bumped straight into Charlie's hard chest.

That was all it took to ignite the fire.

Chapter 19

Gisella and Charlie came together in a flurry of movements. He yanked her dress down from her shoulders, and she pulled his shirt over his head before attacking his belt and pants. They were hot and ravenous for each other's taste.

Charlie leaned her back and stooped his head low and tore at her lacy bra with his teeth. She whimpered when he managed to suck her enlarged and erect nipple into his mouth.

Together they crumpled to the floor.

Charlie's mouth roamed from breast to breast while his hands explored the rest of her. Every move and stroke inflamed her passion and made her greedy for more.

This was what she wanted. This was what she needed.

Charlie didn't know what was happening to him, but he sure as hell was going to enjoy it. As his lips brushed and his fingers touched, he could feel himself fall deeper and deeper into an abyss. Nothing pleased him more to see that her beautiful nipples were, indeed, the color of brown sugar and tasted just as sweet.

"Oh, Gisella." He sucked in a ragged breath. "What are you doing to me?"

"Th-the cake."

He was sure he misunderstood her and continued to travel down her body until he was dragging off her panties with his teeth. Once he'd cleared them from her ankles, he tossed them across the room where he was sure they had landed over a lampshade.

As he climbed back up her body, he had a breathtaking view of the small spring of curls between her legs. He glided upward, raining tiny kisses along the way. When he reached her center, the scent of strawberries overwhelmed him and caused his mouth to water.

"Open up for me, baby," he instructed hoarsely.

Slowly, her knees lowered and pointed in opposite directions. Charlie's erection threatened to punch a hole through the floor when he took two fingers and spread her brown lips to see her luscious cherry pulsing like a heartbeat.

Like a moth to a flame, Charlie dove in, lips first, and sapped her glistening juices.

"Ooh, Ch-Charlie."

Gisella's head rocked from side to side while every limb quivered and writhed. Where it was hot before, the room now encroached on being sweltering. Her body forgot how to breathe. When his tongue made lazy circles, she would pant, but when his tongue would dip in deep, she would hold her breath until she was ready to pass out from the pleasure or simply from lack of oxygen.

To add to the merciless torture, Charlie eased in one finger and then two while his tongue just focused on polishing her clit. His fingers began to stroke, and Gisella lost all ability to think.

She could only feel.

"Damn, baby. You taste so good," Charlie praised and went back to his real dessert.

Her hands roamed over his head and then her fingers dug into his broad shoulders. Then with little warning, her body exploded. At least that was what it felt like. Surely, she had shattered into a million pieces.

Charlie left her lying on the floor, her body quivering from aftershocks to search for his pants. "Please let there be a condom in here. Please," he begged.

God answered his prayers.

He ripped open the packet and sheathed his large erection before crawling back toward her like a prowling panther.

Awakening from her daze, Gisella pulled herself up from the floor and with a strong urge to prove that she could give as well as she could take. In the end her strong panther gave little resistance when she directed him to "lie back."

Charlie's hazel green eyes lit with undeniable lust while his lips curled into a grateful smile. What a woman, he thought when she climbed on top.

"I hope you forgive me in the morning," she said.

Again, Charlie didn't understand her meaning. Whatever it was, he was more than happy to talk to her about it…in the morning.

Gisella eased down, inch by glorious inch. Charlie sucked in his breath, thinking her inner muscles were going to milk the life out of him before they really got started. When she had at last taken in every inch of him, she nearly caused his eyes to roll out the back of his head when her hips rolled in perfect circles.

"Oh, baby."

"You like that?" she purred.

Like it? He loved it. He tried to speak again, but found the job nearly impossible.

The circles were replaced with a gentle back-and-forth action. Then she set a nice rhythm where she combined the two. Words tumbled out of Charlie's mouth, but he doubted that they made much sense. He just didn't want her to stop.

Charlie's hands glided over her hips and then climbed up to cup and squeeze her full breasts. Her nipples were hard as marbles pressing against his palms. Even that turned him on.

To up the ante, Gisella started to bounce. Charlie's hands fell away to grip her hips again. Soon the sound of their bodies slapping against each other filled the room. Wanting to double her pleasure, Charlie's hands continued to roam until they slid in between their moving bodies.

Her rhythm faltered when the pads of his fingers rubbed against her clit. And just like that, he was back in control.

Stars danced behind Gisella's closed eyelids. The sound of her rushing blood roared in her ears.

"You coming, baby?" he asked softly.

She couldn't speak as he rolled her onto her back. He hiked her legs over his shoulders and braced his weight on his folded knees.

"Hmm? You coming?"

Awkwardly, she nodded.

"Wait for me," he instructed. "I'm going to come with you." He folded over and took one of her bouncing nipples into his mouth.

Charlie's lips roamed over one luscious curve after another as he tried to sink deeper into the nectar of this sweet honeycomb. Yet, no matter how long or hard he stroked, he couldn't seem to reach his destination. Sure, she matched his rhythm and at times accelerated past him, but he would always catch up.

He wanted…no, he *needed* more from her.

He shook the bizarre thought from his head and then lost himself in the low melodious moans spilling from her lips. Even her voice was an aphrodisiac, he realized as sweat beaded his forehead, and his hands kneaded her soft, round breasts.

Harder.

Faster.

Her muscles tightened into a smooth sheath and Charlie's breath hitched in anticipation. Ecstasy was just a few strokes away. He could feel it.

"You ready, baby?"

In answer, she cried out his name.

In the next heartbeat, a white light flash behind his eyes and his body exploded as he growled against her shoulder. A calm and something undeniable filled his heart.

"Gisella," he whispered, closing his eyes and gathering her close. "I love you, baby."

Chapter 20

"You drugged me?" Charlie asked, chuckling.

Gisella glanced down where Charlie lay between her breasts. "Not exactly," she hedged. "It was more like a... stimulant."

"Oh, really?" His eyes twinkled.

"No different than if I'd served you a plate of oysters."

"I don't know what kind of oysters you eat over in France, but that cake could put Viagra out of business." He laughed while lazily rolling her puckered nipples between the pads of his fingers.

Gisella smiled as her eyes fluttered closed so she could enjoy the wondrous sensations her man stirred within her. They had made love for most of the night. Both were surprised and pleased by each other's stamina and, judging by what she was feeling rising against her leg, they were far from being done.

"Are you upset?"

"What, for seducing me?" He laughed. "Oh, yeah, I'm *real* mad about that." He climbed her body and pinned her hands above her head. "I better hold you here so you're not tempted to lure more unsuspecting men here with that dangerous chocolate." Charlie's eyes lit up. "You wouldn't happen to have a pair of handcuffs lying around, would you? That could be fun."

Giggling, Gisella tried to buck him off of her. "Well, I had to do something. I was getting tired of taking cold showers."

"Aww. Do I make you horny, baby?" Charlie asked in his best Austin Powers impression.

She tried to reach a pillow so she could hit him with it, but only succeeded in rocking against him even more. She finally went still when she felt the head of his morning erection against the apex of her sex.

He snickered. "So you *do* know how to behave. Good to know." He slid his cock back and forth along the top of her clit.

Gisella's eyes glazed with desire.

"You want to know why I resisted making love to you before last night?" he asked.

Their gazes locked.

"Because from the moment I saw you, I knew that you were special, and I wanted to treat you as such. I didn't want just one thing from you. I wanted *everything*."

A tide of emotion swelled within Gisella. "I want everything, too." Tears trickled from the corner of her eyes.

Charlie smiled. "I meant what I said last night."

She blinked up.

"I love you." He leaned forward and brushed his lips across hers. "I've never said that to any other woman."

Gisella's vision blurred as her tears became a flood. "I love you, too."

"Does that mean you'll marry me?"

She nodded vigorously, not having to think twice on her answer.

Charlie's smile stretched as he finally dipped his hips and entered her in one smooth stroke.

Gisella gasped and then wrapped her long limbs around his waist. At the feel of his deep, long and steady strokes, she thrashed her head among the pillows. She didn't know how much more she could take, but there was one thing she knew for sure—heaven indeed existed on earth.

He released her hands, and she quickly glided them around his broad shoulders and then dug her short nails into moist skin. While their bodies rocked, their mouths locked and sealed their souls together.

This wasn't sex.

This was making love.

They wanted this moment in time to last forever, but as their bodies' friction drove them to higher planes, a familiar and powerful sensation tried to rob them of breath.

Feverish, she couldn't understand the words tumbling from his lips. But seconds before her orgasm detonated, Charlie's words were clear.

"IloveyouIloveyouIloveyouIloveyouIloveyouIloveyou."

With those words ringing in her ears, Gisella came.

* * *

"I'm glad you're back," Nicole said, leading the march behind Anna as she entered her apartment. "You need to nip this whole Charlie Masters thing in the bud."

Anna shook her head. "Believe me. I'm going to have a loooong talk with her."

Nicole sucked her teeth. "I tried that, but Ms. Thang told me how grown she was and that she made her own decisions. I *told* you Charlie was going to be on her like white on rice. Now didn't I?"

"Sho did," Emmadonna co-signed.

"Well, she is a consenting adult," Jade added in her pip-squeak voice.

The three women stopped in the apartment's entry-way, turned and looked at Jade as if her middle name was Judas.

"What? I'm just stating a fact."

Emmadonna settled her hands on her thick hips. "Charlie is a dog. That's a fact, too."

"Amen," Anna and Nicole praised.

"Just like it's a fact Em lied when she said she'd slept with him."

"I never said that," Emmadonna said.

"You did, too."

"Ladies," Nicole interrupted. "Focus."

Anna turned around and nearly tripped over Sasha. "Hey, baby," she cooed and then glanced up at the table. "What the hell? Is she starting a floral shop now, too?" she asked, noting the large vase of roses.

"Hmmph. We're probably too late," Nicole said. "He's

had her all to himself for a month. That's more than enough time for him to have the girl whipped."

"A month," Anna said. "I've been calling her at least every other day, and she hadn't said a word."

"Like I said…" Nicole snapped an imaginary whip.

"Since when does Charlie date someone for a month?" Anna said. "He doesn't *do* relationships. Remember?"

Jade shrugged. "Maybe it's serious."

Again, the three women stared at her.

"What?"

Anna rolled her eyes and walked away. She didn't get far. The sight of dirty dishes and an open bottle of wine left on the dining room table snagged her attention. "What the hell?"

"Hmm. Looks like someone had a hot date last night," Nicole said.

Anna walked away from her rollaway luggage to check out the living room. Half-empty glasses of wine were left on the coffee table, but it was the lampshade that drew everyone's eye.

"What the…is that what I think it is?" Emmadonna said.

"Interesting place to hang your panties," Jade snickered.

Anna kicked a pair of male slacks on the floor and then bent to pick up the wallet that was hidden underneath.

"Any bets on who the mystery man is?" Nicole asked.

Anna hadn't realized that she was holding her breath until she flipped open the leather wallet and stared at Charles Masters's driver's license. "I'm going to kill him."

Charlie discovered that Gisella was ticklish. Not just a little, but extremely ticklish—and just about everywhere.

"Stop, stop, stop," she begged while whacking him over the head with a pillow.

He had no intentions of stopping. He attacked under her arms, her sides and a few times on the soles of her feet. "Who's the best?" he taunted. "Tell me who's the best."

"No!"

Bam! Bam! Bam!

Gisella's bedroom door rattled on its hinges, instantly ending the lovers' naked horseplay.

"Gisella, I need to talk to you!"

"Anna," Gisella gasped.

"I guess that means she's back home," Charlie said.

"Hide! She can't see you."

"I know Charlie's in there," Anna said, letting them know she could hear them.

"Yeah, we know he's in there," Nicole chimed.

Gisella groaned.

"Strange echo," Charlie said.

"It's the Lonely Hearts girls," Gisella muttered.

"Whoa. I don't do groups."

Grabbing a pillow, she whacked him on the head and watched him fall back in a dramatic death scene. "Will you stop playing? We gotta do something."

"What? She knows I'm in here." He shrugged and then folded one arm behind his head.

For not taking the situation serious, Gisella gave him one good shove and flipped him over the edge of the bed. He landed with a loud thud and then quickly popped his head up.

Gisella slapped a hand over her mouth to stop herself from laughing.

"When we're married, I won't put up with domestic violence from you."

"Gisella!"

Bam! Bam! Bam!

"Hide in the bathroom," she directed, scrambling out of bed and wrapping the top sheet around her body. "Take a shower or something."

He frowned. "What, are you ashamed of me now?"

Why was he being so difficult? "Please," she begged.

"Oh, all right." Charlie struggled to his feet, but when he took two steps he had to grab hold of the bed.

"Are you all right?"

"Just a little dizzy," he chuckled. "Must have gotten up too fast." He stood again and walked a crooked line to the bathroom.

She watched him, frowning, until her sister continued to shout her name. "I'm coming," she snapped and stomped toward the door. When she cracked it open, Anna looked like she was ready to breathe fire. "Yes?"

"What are you doing," she hissed.

Gisella cocked her head. "Surely, it hasn't been *that* long for you."

Anna sucked in a breath. "You're making a *big* mistake." She shoved Gisella and Charlie's clothes through the door. "That man is nothing more than a roaming dog searching for a place to bury his bone."

Gisella laughed. "Did you come up with that on your own?"

Her sister glared. "Trust me. He'll only break your heart."

"Why, because he broke yours?" she challenged. At Anna's stricken look, she tried to apologize. "Anna—"

"So he told you?"

"Told her what?" Emmadonna planted her nose into the conversation.

The sisters stared at one another. After a long pause, Anna's voice dropped into a trembling whisper. "That was a long time ago. I thought…we were just friends."

"It's not important," Gisella said, matching her sister's tone. "He actually came here last month looking for you. Said something about wanting to apologize—"

"Look, Gisella. What happened or didn't happen between us in college doesn't matter. What matters is his reputation. He doesn't stick around. He never has, and he never will."

"It's not like that with us."

Nicole chimed up. "Girl, do you know how many women have thought that?"

"Nicole," Anna snapped. "This is an A-and-B conversation. Will you please C your way out of it?"

"Let's just talk about this later," Gisella said.

The shower came on in the bathroom.

Her sister crossed her arms. "I want him out of here."

"No."

Anna's brows arched. "What?"

"I pay rent. This is my apartment, too, and I say he stays."

"Gisella…"

"I love him." Judging by the pain that stretched across her sister's face, one would have thought Gisella had stabbed her. "And he loves me."

Anna jabbed a hand onto her hip. "What? He told you that?"

"As a matter of fact, he did. So you might as well get used to seeing him around…because we're getting married." Before any of them could respond to that, Gisella firmly closed the door in their faces.

Charlie stood beneath the shower's steady water flow with his arms braced against the tile. He waited for this latest wave of vertigo to pass. The episodes were happening more often and were frankly scaring the hell out of him.

The test. He needed to take the test.

He shook his head, confused as to what he was doing. How could he possibly be making plans to marry Gisella when he didn't know what the future held?

He was being selfish.

"So what if you are?" the devil on his shoulder asked. "What's wrong with grabbing hold of a little happiness before you kick the bucket?"

The angel on his right refuted that. "You have to tell her the truth."

"No way, José," the devil said. "Who wants to deal with all that crying?"

Charlie thought about all the women he'd spent the last month calling, seeking and hoping to give closure to any open-ended issues. How easy it had been to tell *them* he was dying. But the woman he loved? He shook his head.

I can't tell her.

"Mind if I join you in there?"

Charlie turned toward Gisella's smiling face and felt his strength return. "I can always use a good back scrubber."

In the shower, Charlie and Gisella spent more time being dirty than getting clean. It wasn't until the water heater gave out and started pelting icicles on them did they finally scramble to get out.

Dried and dressed, Gisella's stomach rumbled. "I'm starving. We already missed breakfast. You want to head down to Oscar's for some lunch?" she asked.

"Sure, but for future reference, this brother can always eat."

She laughed. "I'll keep that in mind." She started toward the door and stopped. "Aww, damn." She sighed. "I know those ladies are still out there, ready to pounce."

"C'mon." He kissed her on the cheek. "Just ignore them."

When they left the bedroom, it was just as Gisella suspected. The women were all sitting in the living room, casting evil glares their way.

"We're going to head out and get something to eat," Gisella said. "Can we bring you anything back?"

Anna kept her mouth clamped while stroking Sasha's thick fur.

Nicole, Emmadonna and Jade were steady fanning themselves.

Gisella's eyes fell to the small plates with unmistakable chocolate crumbs. "Um, did you eat some of that cake in the dining room?"

Anna sighed. "They did. I didn't have much of an appetite."

"Um, hmm. It was good, too."

The women licked their lips and eyeballed Charlie with blatant desire.

"God, it's hot in here," Nicole panted.

Gisella spun around, grabbed Charlie's hand and yelled, "Run, Charlie. Run."

Chapter 21

Life was beautiful.

Gisella had never been happier. Charlie had filled the past three weeks with love and infused her night with passion. There were plenty of times she thought she should be ashamed of just how insatiable she was when it came to their lovemaking.

She no longer made *Amour Chocolat* cake, but she did alter the recipe to make truffles—with a little less potency and with a big warning label. The result: business had quadrupled. She and Isabella had to hire more employees and were now considering opening a second shop out in the suburbs.

"Godiva, eat your heart out," Isabella sassed as she rung up another sale.

Gisella laughed and turned her attention to the next customer in line. "May I help you?" she asked.

The woman smiled. "Well, hello."

Gisella cocked her head at the familiar face and struggled for a name.

"It's Lexi," she said.

Gisella remembered the woman from the restaurant. "Oh, *bonjour.*"

"I see you still have that cute little accent."

"Just like you still have yours," Gisella said, wondering what this woman really wanted.

"Charming," she said. "I can see why Charlie has taken an interest in you. He always did like women who were…different. How *are* things going with you and Charlie?"

Isabella turned from the register and eyed the woman.

"He's wonderful. As always," Gisella said, determined to remain pleasant.

"I hear you two are still dating?"

"From whom?"

The woman shrugged. "Around. Atlanta may be a big city, but in a lot of ways it's very small. It's not hard to get information when you really want it."

"I have no idea," Gisella said. "I don't spy on people. I think it's tacky." Her growing irritation only seemed to amuse Lexi.

"Humph. I hope you don't believe that you're actually going to nail Charlie down or get him in front of a preacher." Lexi plopped a thick book on the counter.

"What's that?"

"Charlie's little black book. It has all the names of all

the women he's ever…dated. I'm sure they'll be more than happy to talk to you."

"And how did you get it?"

"I have my ways," she smirked. "Let me tell you some-thing, sweetheart. You're no different from anybody else. In time, he'll get bored, and he'll dump you like he's dumped *all* the rest. It's what he does."

"What in the hell do you mean you're getting married?" Taariq roared.

Everyone in Herman's barbershop stopped what they were doing and swiveled their necks toward the Kappa Psi Kappa brothers.

Charlie slouched down in Herman's chair, surprised by their reaction. "Damn, y'all. My name isn't H. F. Hutton."

Suddenly they all tried to talk at one time. Questions like, "Are you crazy?", "Have you lost your mind?" and "What the heck have you been smoking?" were tossed at him.

Herman was the most amused. He clapped and rubbed his old leathery hands together. "Lawd. Lawd. Lawd. You still performing miracles."

Charlie rolled his eyes. "This hardly qualifies as a miracle."

A light flashed, temporarily blinding Charlie. He looked up to see Bobby aiming his camera phone at him. "What are you doing?"

"Capturing this historical moment. I'm putting this up on my Facebook and Myspace page. I think I'm going to title it 'The Death of a Playa'."

"Very funny."

"Well, who's the lucky girl?" Hylan asked, frowning. "I didn't even know you were seeing anyone serious."

"I think I know," Derrick said. He sat smiling in the barber chair across from Charlie. "Gisella Jacobs."

"Who?" All the men in the barbershop chorused.

"You know. The woman Isabella hired to make his birthday cake for his party."

"The one she went into business with?" Hylan asked.

"Yep."

"Damn, bro." Taariq folded his arms. "That must have been one hell of a cake."

Hylan scoffed. "You probably need to check the ingredients. She probably put roots on you."

Charlie chuckled, remembering Gisella's *Amour Chocolat* cake.

J.T. stopped hawking his CDs for a moment to agree. "Yeah. I heard about chicks like that. Is she Creole? You know a Creole woman will put the roots on you in a heartbeat. My grandmother said that one stole her third husband like that. Fixed him a bowl of gumbo, and he was out the door."

Charlie sighed and wondered why he'd bothered to say anything. It probably had a lot to do with him just being happy as hell. For the past three weeks, he and Gisella had spent every free moment together making love. In fact, he would much rather be home with her now than sitting here jaw-jacking with this group of knuckleheads.

Herman patted Charlie on the shoulder. "Tell us something about your little lady. When are you going to bring her by here so we can get a good look at her?"

Bobby smirked. "I bet she's fine. My man Charlie here only strolls with the finest chicks. Ain't that right?" He looked at Charlie. "She's fine, ain't she?"

Herman clucked his tongue, a signal that he was annoyed with his great grandson. "That's exactly why you're going to fall in love with a big cockeyed woman. God gonna get you back for always trying to judge with just your eyes."

Bobby shuddered at the thought. The other men laughed.

Herman went back to edging Charlie's sides. "Well, I'm proud of you, son. I know your daddy would be proud of you, too."

Charlie smiled. "Thanks, old man."

"I guess it's true what they say. When one door closes another one opens," Taariq said.

Charlie glared.

"What?" Taariq eyed him suspiciously. "Don't tell me you haven't told her."

The rest of the Kappa boys frowned. "Told her what?"

"Nothing," Charlie said, hoping Taariq would catch the hint and let the matter drop.

He didn't. "Far be it from me to tell you how to run your business…"

"Then don't."

"But keeping secrets is no one way to start off a marriage—or even an engagement."

"True. True," Herman chimed.

Stanley scratched his head, looking lost. "What? Are you talking about him being broke and filing for bankruptcy?"

Charlie jaw clenched. "You told them?"

Taariq didn't bother to look contrite. "It slipped out."

"I swear you guys are the worst kind of gossipers."

Hylan held up his hand. "Heeey. We don't gossip. We *share* information. Totally different from gossiping. Women gossip."

Everyone in the shop nodded at that assessment.

Derrick didn't. "That has to be the most sexist thing I've ever heard."

"Chill out, D.," Hylan said. "Isabella isn't here." He returned his attention to Charlie. "You know you can't marry a woman without telling her you're broke."

"Especially a sista," Taariq agreed.

J.T. stumbled over and opened his merchandise-laden raincoat. "Well if you're looking for something on the cheap, I can hook you up. I got a couple of rings that looks one hundred percent zirconium. She'll never know the difference."

Charlie cracked up. "J.T., get out of my face with that crap, man. I'm not trying to put something on her finger that's going to turn green. Are you crazy?"

"Nah. Nah. Check it out. What you do is, every night when she goes to sleep, you just slip the ring off and put a tiny coat of clear nail polish on it. She'll never know."

The men laughed.

"Man, please. You stand a better chance of me buying some socks from you."

"Whoa. Whoa. I got some out in the car. Hold up. I'll be right back."

Charlie looked at his friends. "That brother got issues."

"Yeah, but he drives a Mercedes," Bobby said.

"An '82," Charlie countered.

"A Mercedes is a Mercedes. Somebody's rich butt sat in it at one time." Bobby handed a mirror to the nervous customer sitting in his seat.

It was the first time Charlie thought the young barber had actually done a decent job.

"All right, Hylan. You're next," Bobby said as his customer climbed out of his chair.

"Boy, please. I'm not about to have you messing up my head."

Insulted, Bobby frowned. "But you're bald. How am I gonna mess up your head?"

"Yeah. Well, I want to remain bald, not scalp-less."

Another round of laughter ensued.

"Y'all wrong, man." Bobby shook his head. "Y'all wrong for that."

Herman turned off his clippers and then folded his arms. "So when is the big day?" he asked, bringing the conversation back to Charlie.

At this point, Charlie knew that he should keep his mouth shut, but good news was hard to keep to oneself. "I bought the ring this morning. I plan on giving it to her this evening. If all goes right, I might be looking at wedding in the next couple of weeks."

"A couple of weeks?" the shop clamored.

"What's the damn rush?" Taariq asked. "Her daddy got a shotgun after you or something?"

"Hardly."

Still mystified, Taariq kept shaking his head. "Whatever happened to long engagements? You know, date a couple of years, and then be engaged for a couple of more."

"She's a woman," Charlie said. "Not a bottle of wine."

"Yeah, man. That's not how it works," Derrick said laughing. "When it's love, you instantly know. All that stalling and dragging your feet is just a brother fighting it."

"Ain't nothing wrong with a good fight," Bobby interjected.

Taariq pointed at the young man. "See, now even the rookie is talking sense."

Bobby proudly puffed out his chest.

"Nah. I think my man, Derrick, is right on this one. When it's right, you know," Charlie said.

Herman sighed. "Y'all gonna get an old man crying up in here. I'm so proud. I've been cutting Charlie's head long before he even knew what to do with a girl. Now to see this new level of maturity, it just does my heart good."

It was Charlie's turn to puff out his chest.

Herman brushed off Charlie's neck and removed the smock.

Charlie handed him a folded bill and stood up from his chair. "Well, boys," he said, thinking about the ring he had waiting for Gisella. "I'm going to go make it official tonight. Wish me luck."

Taariq, Hylan, Stanley and Bobby grumbled.

Derrick and Herman boomed a clear, "Good luck."

Laughing, Charlie slapped his hand down on Taariq's shoulder. "Get the marbles out of your mouths and dust off your tux."

"I'll believe it when I see you at an altar," Taariq said.

Charlie shook his head and started toward the door. He'd

taken only a few steps before pain exploded in his head and the room spun beneath his feet.

"Charlie?" Derrick called out.

Charlie dropped like a stone and banged his head on the floor.

"Someone call 9-1-1!"

Chapter 22

"Welcome back to the land of the living," Dr. Weiner said, smiling. "You gave everyone quite a scare."

Charlie groaned. His head felt as if someone had taken an axe to it and had a damn good time. When he moved, pain exploded at the back of his head and forced him to collapse back onto the pillow.

"Easy, now," Dr. Weiner warned. "We don't want you to overdo it."

Charlie wasn't going to argue. He closed his eyes to retreat from the room's bright light and exhaled a long breath.

"Your friends tell me that you took a rather nasty fall."

Had he? He couldn't remember. He opened his mouth to speak but his parched throat grated like sandpaper. "W-water."

"Hold on a second." Weiner turned toward the desk next to the hospital bed and poured a glass of water. "Here you go," he said, tipping the cup toward Charlie's lips.

It was the best water Charlie had ever tasted. He drained the plastic cup in less than two seconds. "More."

The doctor complied and then said, "I have to ask you a few questions. They may sound silly to you, but I need to make sure there hasn't been any bruising or severe brain injury from your fall. Can you tell me your name?"

"Ch-Charles Masters," he whispered.

"Very good." Weiner retrieved a pin light from his breast pocket and the flashed it into Charlie's eyes to check their dilation. "What day is it?"

"Saturday," Charlie answered, trying not to be irritated by such mundane questions.

"Do you remember what happened?" Weiner asked.

At first, nothing came to mind, but after concentrating, bits and pieces of images surfaced. "Yeah, I—I think so."

"What do you remember?"

Charlie pushed himself through the pain of talking. "Barbershop. My head started hurting. I got dizzy. Fell."

Dr. Weiner nodded. "I'm going to order an MRI, but I believe you have a grade three concussion. We should probably keep you here overnight for observation. You'll live…for now."

Charlie's eyes fluttered open.

"While I have you here—"

"No."

A long silence followed. Dr. Weiner's hands gripped the bed's steel railing. "Charlie, you're making a grave mistake."

"It's mine to make," he countered. He glanced away when angry tears stung the backs of his eyes. "I—if I am sick, I don't want to spend what time I have left running in and out of hospitals."

"I've always known that you were hard-headed, Charlie, but I'd hoped that cracking your head open had knocked some sense into you." He paused. "I saw the look on your friends' faces out there. They care a lot about you. Have you thought about how they're going to feel when they find out you kept this illness from them?"

Charlie ground his jaw in stubborn silence. The last thing he wanted was a sermon.

"You have a responsibility to those you love. That includes telling them the truth. No matter how painful."

Charlie closed his eyes again and was greeted with the image of Gisella lying in his bed of satin sheets and smiling seductively. How could he tell her he was dying after he had allowed her to believe they were preparing for a future together?

"You're being selfish."

So what? Why couldn't he grab happiness while he still had a chance? Charlie pressed a hand against his forehead, but no matter how hard he fought against it, the doctor's words seeped into his thick skull.

"I'm not going to lie to you. You're at a major cross-road," Weiner continued. "It's not up to me to judge. You have to make your own decisions. But I gotta tell you, I think you're making the wrong ones."

Charlie's picture of Gisella then changed into one of his mother greeting him Tuesday nights with a kiss and then one of him and his Kappa brothers laughing it up every Saturday morning at Herman's and then his thoughts returned to Gisella.

"All right. All right. I'll take your damn test," Charlie snapped.

Weiner drew and released a satisfied breath. "I'll order for a nurse to come take you upstairs. The test won't take but a few minutes."

"Now?"

"I'm not giving you a chance to back out of this… again."

Gisella stared at Charlie's little black book.

She wasn't going to call anyone. What was the point? The women listed in there were all a part of his past. She was his future.

Right?

It was a good pep talk. One that worked for the first hour, but by the second, third and even the fourth, those words started to have a hollow ring. Even Lexi's sneering voice refused to stop echoing in her head.

"In time, he'll get bored, and he'll dump you like he's dumped all the rest. It's what he does."

Was she telling the truth? Despite their dating for the last seven weeks, there was still plenty Gisella didn't know about Charlie. How many times had she sensed that he was keeping something from her? How many times had she caught him staring at her with an odd sadness in his eyes? Was he already getting bored? Was a breakup just beyond the horizon?

Yet, there was so much she *did* know—and loved—that had nothing to do with him being good-looking or good in bed—*great in bed*, actually. Charlie was intelligent, loyal to his friends, funny, kind and endearing. There was something about the way he held her that made her feel like the quintessential woman. In his arms, she was sexy, alluring, strong and powerful—all at the same time. With him in her corner, there was nothing she couldn't do. No challenge too hard, no dreams impossible.

How could she *not* fall in love?

Gisella's gaze returned to the little black book. How many other women had felt the same way about Charlie?

"Krista, could you take over?" she asked, removing her apron. "I'm going to head home."

"Sure." Krista smiled. "I don't know how you put in the hours you do anyway."

At home, Gisella's anxieties increased. When she phoned Charlie, all her calls were transferred to his voicemail. If she could just hear his voice maybe she would calm down.

Curled up on the living room sofa with Sasha purring softly on her lap, Gisella stared at the black book as if in a trance. In the last hour, she had thrown the book in the garbage several times only to fish it out minutes later.

"In time, he'll get bored, and he'll dump you like he's dumped all the rest. It's what he does."

There was laughter in the hallway seconds before Anna and the Lonely Hearts breezed into the apartment. Clearly, they'd spent the day shopping, judging by the number of shopping bags. However, they sobered when they spilled into the living room and saw Gisella.

"You're home early," Anna said casually. A clear reflection of how their relationship had been strained since she'd learned about Gisella and Charlie's relationship. "What are you doing?"

"Nothing."

"We can see that," Nicole said. She lowered her bags near the coffee table and plopped on the cushion next to Gisella. "You look like a zombie."

"What's this?" Emmadonna asked picking up the black book and joining them on the couch.

"Charlie's little black book."

The Lonely Hearts gasped.

Nicole snatched the book from Emmadonna's hands. "Girrrl, how did you get your hands on this?"

"You mean men actually have those things?" Jade squeaked.

Excited, Emmadonna grabbed the book back. "Are you going to call any of them? Let's do it now."

"No."

"Where's the phone?"

"I *said* no."

"No?" the women chorused.

"Why the hell not?" Nicole asked.

Still standing in the living room's archway, Anna stared at her sister. "What's the matter, Gisella?"

"Nothing. I—I just…" She shook her head. "I was just thinking."

Anna set her bags down and climbed over her friends' legs and forced them to scoot over so she could sit next Gisella. "Do you want to talk about it?"

Sasha abandoned Gisella's lap for her owner's.

Talk about what? That she had this unexplainable anxiety over a relationship that everyone kept warning her to stay away from? One look at her sister and Gisella could tell that she was just jumping at the bit to say, *I told you so*.

Besides, Charlie hasn't done anything. It was just a feeling that bad news was just around the corner, caused by the seeds that Lexi woman planted in her head.

Gisella forced on a smile and unfolded her legs. "You know what? I think I'm just going go and see my man."

"You mean *everybody's* man, don't you?" Emmadonna thumbed through the pages. "Damn, do you know the mayor is in here?"

Gisella tried to grab the black book. "And I'm giving him his book back."

"Whoa!" The ladies jumped to their feet.

"Let's not be too hasty there," Nicole said. "Apparently, you're too emotional and aren't thinking clearly. You do *not* give a playa his little black book back. That's like giving an recovering alcoholic a bottle of Jack Daniels."

Gisella snatched the book. "No offense, Nicole. But I'll start taking man advice from you when you have one of your own."

Chapter 23

The bone marrow test didn't take long. All that was left for Charlie to do was to wait. But he wasn't going to do that in a hospital. After insisting to be released, the Kappa Psi Kappa brothers drove Charlie back to his apartment. The ride was like a funeral procession. His boys clearly didn't know what to say to him and he certainly didn't know how to get the conversation started.

Once at his apartment, it was odd to see the Kappas, big, strapping manly men, fussing over him like a group of mother hens. Before he knew it, they had him propped up on the sofa with pillows and blankets and arguing who was better qualified to stay and watch for the night.

Derrick suggested calling Mama Arlene, and Charlie threatened him within an inch of his life when he'd picked up the phone. "I'm all right, man. There's no need to worry her. It's just a bump on the head."

Grudgingly, Derrick placed the phone back on the receiver and then shared a look with the other boys.

"Just spit it out," Charlie said.

Taariq crossed his arms. "Actually, we're waiting for you to tell us what's going on. What was up with all that extra testing?"

For a brief moment, Charlie thought that he could downplay the whole situation. "It was nothing. It…" He glanced at their solemn and dubious faces and knew that the jig was up. Time to come clean. "Dr. Weiner thinks I'm dying."

Everyone quickly collapsed into the nearest chair.

"Go on," Hylan said.

Charlie started from the beginning. How he'd gone to the doctor's to prepare for a business trip and ended where he'd finally was cornered into taking the test an hour ago. When he was done, the silence condemned him.

"And this is called a plastic what?" Derrick asked. He scooped out his cell phone so he could search WebMD.

"Aplastic anemia," Charlie repeated. "I didn't *really* believe the diagnosis…until the headaches and dizzy spells. I mean, most of the time I feel fine."

"It's just when you cracked your head on the floor that gave you pause?" Hylan asked.

Stanley looked on the verge of tears. "I don't understand. Why didn't you tell us? I thought we were boys."

Here we go.

"It's complicated, Stan," Charlie said. "I didn't want you guys to start…"

"What?" Derrick folded his arms. "You didn't want us to start what?"

"Treating me different," Charlie said.

"We wouldn't have done that," Stanley protested.

The rest of the Kappas chorused in agreement.

Charlie laughed. "Please. Look at you. I've been in the apartment less than an hour and you guys got me snug as a bug in a rug. Hell, dawgs, a minute ago I was scared one of you were going to stick a thermometer up my butt if I asked for some aspirins."

A couple of them hung their heads in guilt.

"All right. All right," Hylan said. "Maybe we over-reacted. But it was a little disturbing to see you wipe out the way you did at Herman's. You scared us."

"Sorry, man." Charlie shrugged. "I was just trying to do the right thing."

They bobbed their heads, but Stanley was barely keeping it together.

Having pity on him, Charlie said, "C'mon. Let's hug it out real quick." He stood and the Kappas came together for one big group hug and then broke away as if the incident never happened.

"But why would you call old girlfriends and tell *them?*" Hylan asked.

"Trying to bring closure to whichever one of them van-dalized my car and trashed my apartment. Whoever it is is still messing with me. Things keep disappearing around here."

"Should've listened to Herman," Derrick said, waving

his finger. "He warned you about being out of the field too long. Look at you now. You're in the middle of some fatal attraction soap opera." He glanced at his other brothers. "It's gonna happen to you guys too. Watch."

Hylan rolled his eyes. "Can we save the preaching for Sundays?" He turned to Charlie. "So where does all this "I'm getting married" stuff fit in? Does your girl know about all this—or are you keeping this from her just like the whole bankruptcy thing?"

It was on the tip of Charlie's tongue to tell the guys that it was none of their business what he did and didn't tell Gisella, but he hesitated too long and they had their answer.

"Man, what the hell are you thinking?" Derrick exploded out of his chair. "Are you really that damn selfish? How are you going to marry someone and *not* tell her you may be dying?"

Hylan was equally outraged. "Bump that. Do you even really love this girl or are you just swept up in the moment because you think you're getting ready to kick the bucket?"

The accusation had Charlie jumping to his feet. "What the hell kind of question is that? Of course I love her!"

Stanley, who was still hunched over in his chair, calmly asked, "Are you sure?"

"Damn right I'm sure." Charlie's face twisted in disgust. "Gisella is the best thing that has ever happened to me."

Taariq shrugged. "But you have to admit it's a little convenient your falling in love at the twelfth hour. *You,* a man who ran only second to Wilt Chamberlain in the number of women he'd slept with, finds the love of his life the moment he finds out he's dying. Do you know what the odds are on that?"

Charlie blinked.

Taariq shook his head. "C'mon, dawg. Who are you fooling? Us? Or yourself?"

"Or Gisella?" Derrick added.

Charlie opened his mouth to protest…but no words came out.

Gisella arrived at Charlie's high-rise apartment with her heart in her throat. In just a few minutes she would see Charlie, and all the anxieties of the day would melt away. At least that's what she was hoping. She waved at Todd at the security desk as she headed toward the elevator bay.

At Charlie's door she elected to knock first instead of using the key he'd insisted on giving her. The last person she expected to answer the door was Isabella's husband. "Derrick?" She blinked up at him and then tried to glance around his large shoulders. "What are you doing here?"

"Hey, Gisella," he said, looking equally caught off guard. After a beat of silence, she wondered whether he intended to let her in.

"Is Charlie here?"

"Who? Oh, Charlie. Yeah. Um, come on in." He finally stepped back from the door.

Gisella gave him an awkward laugh before crossing into the apartment. The surprises continued when she found Charlie in the living room propped up on pillows and surrounded by three other guys.

"Gisella," Charlie said, standing. "I didn't know you were coming by."

Her curious gaze darted around the men's strange expressions.

"Oh. Um. You remember the guys from the birthday party. This here is Hylan, Taariq and Stanley," he said, touching each one on the shoulder.

"Hello," they greeted her, smiling.

"Bonjour."

"And of course you remember Derrick there."

Every fiber in her being told her something was wrong. The men were acting like she was an undercover cop who'd just busted them on an illegal act.

After the introductions were done, the silence in the room became a living, breathing thing.

Finally, Derrick broke the silence by clapping his hands together. "Well, I guess we'll be heading out."

It sounded more like a command than a suggestion. The other Kappa brothers quickly agreed and gathered their belongings. The situation made Gisella feel as if she should be apologizing for breaking up the private party.

"It was nice meeting you," Stanley said as he filed past her.

She nodded weakly as they all headed out.

"Bobby was right. She *is* fine," one of them whispered.

Both she and Charlie remained silent until they heard the front door close. "They seem nice," she said, easing into the room, trying to break the ice.

Gisella knew the Kappa boys more by the stories Charlie and Isabella shared with her than anything else. Her gaze took in the pillows and blankets spread out on the sofa again. "Camping out?"

"Sort of," he said sheepishly. "I, uh, sort of had an accident at the barbershop today. Hit my head. Got a concussion."

"What?" She instantly flew to him and tried to examine him for herself.

Charlie stopped her by taking her hands into his and kissing them. "It's all right. It's going to take more than a cement floor to bust open this head."

She laughed and until that moment, didn't realize how much she needed to do that. "That must be why I was so worried about you today," she said in relief. "I kept having this bad vibe ever since…" She shook her head and allowed Charlie to lead her to sit down and pull her into his arms. "I had the strangest visit from that Lexi woman, and I can't believe I let her get into my head."

He frowned. "Lexi?"

Gisella opened her purse and pulled out Charlie's black book. "She brought me this."

"What?" Charlie removed his arm from around her and took the book. "Lexi?" He shook his head as his rising anger caused visible lines along his jaw. "I should have known." He slammed the book on the table.

"She suggested that I call—"

"And did you?" he snapped.

"Of course not! I would never do that." She paused. "But it's a thick book."

"So?" He stood up and started pacing.

She blinked at him. "So…I didn't really realize how many women you had in your life."

"What…you wanted a number?"

Now Gisella jumped to her feet. "I never said I wanted a number, I'm just saying you've slept with a lot of women—even the mayor is in there!"

"Oh, so you read it?"

"No. Nicole—"

"Nicole? You let your *friends* read my personal property?"

"Nicole is not…" She stopped and drew a deep breath. "Okay. Are you purposely trying to start a fight with me?"

He stopped pacing long enough to breathe fire toward her. After a long minute passed, he finally glanced away. He didn't know if he could go through with this. After talking to the Kappas, he was suddenly confused on so many things.

Gisella forced herself to calm down. When she glanced back at him, she remembered his concussion. "Let's just drop this. Clearly, Lexi gave me the book for this very thing to happen." She smiled and walked over to him. "But I'm not going anywhere, baby. In fact, I'm going to take care of you tonight. We'll stay in, and I'll cook us something to eat and we can sit here on the couch and watch a movie." She kissed his cheek. "Would you like that?"

Charlie eased away.

Gisella's heart dropped. "What's wrong?"

"Nothing." He shrugged. "What makes you think something is wrong?" he asked, avoiding eye contact. He couldn't believe he was about to do this, but maybe everyone was right. Up until now, he was being selfish, planning a future when he didn't have one and wanting her to fall in love with him when he was just going to break her heart. Was this what the song meant when it said, if you love someone set them free?

Gisella studied him and was convinced that she could literally see the wheels in his head spinning. In that moment everything became clear.

"You want to break up with me," she said simply.

He looked at her then.

She waited for him to deny the accusation.

And waited.

And waited.

"I see." She shook her head and grabbed her purse from couch. "You know, you're a real piece of work."

"Gisella—"

"Save it. You've already wasted enough of my time." She stomped away from him and marched toward the door steadily cursing him out in French. If he thought for a second that she was going to throw some temper tantrum, he had another thing coming. So intent on her leaving, she was caught off guard when he grabbed her wrist. "Gisella." He spun her around.

Out of reflex, she slapped him. "Drop dead."

Chapter 24

"Mission accomplished," Lexi murmured under her breath. It didn't take a rocket scientist to know that the look on Gisella's face when she stormed toward her car in the high-rise parking deck meant one thing: everything had gone exactly as planned.

Now she felt vindicated. Of course she still had one more bomb set in motion, but she had no doubt that when all was said and done, Charlie Masters would learn a valuable lesson.

Gisella slammed her car door and revved the engine. A second later, tires squealed, and a cloud of white smoke jetted out of her exhaust pipe when she peeled out of the parking deck. To Lexi's surprise, she experienced a nugget of sympathy but quickly shook it off. "Trust me, Frenchie. I did you a favor."

* * *

Charlie leaned his head against the front door while the left side of his face still throbbed from Gisella's powerful slap. He felt as low as a man could get. Now Gisella believed that she was no different than the already forgotten faces and names in his damn black book.

He squeezed his eyes tight, but tears still managed to escape and race down his face. This morning he was looking forward to officially proposing to Gisella. He would have never believed that the day would end with her hating his guts and with him hating himself.

The only thing that prevented him from running after her was Dr. Weiner and his frat brothers' words. He couldn't continue to be selfish. It wasn't fair. However, there was one thing he now knew for sure—he was definitely in love with Gisella. It wasn't fear of fading mortality. The gut-wrenching sickness he experienced now could only be love.

Somehow he managed to pull himself away from the door. Seconds later, he was in his bedroom pulling out the small royal-blue box from the top nightstand drawer. Before he could open it, he eased down on the edge of the bed and held his breath.

Ready, Charlie opened the box and stared at the elegant two-carat princess-cut diamond ring. Now he would have to continue to use his imagination of how the ring would've looked on Gisella's finger. After a long while, he finally exhaled and accepted the pain in his heart. It was worse than anything he'd ever experienced.

He lay back on the bed and wondered how long he would have to endure. Surely it would ease soon. *Please, Lord, let it ease soon.*

"A plastic what?" Isabella asked her husband. It was late and they were getting ready for bed when he dropped this bombshell on her.

"Aplastic anemia," Derrick repeated. "The whole thing is messed up," he said worriedly. The idea of losing not only his best friend but a man who was like his brother was hard to wrap his brain around. "We're all waiting for his test results. It can take up to seven to ten days. Until then, we're not to breathe a word…not even to Mama Arlene."

Isabella's heart ached for her husband. She loved Charlie. He was like family. And seeing him so happy these past two months had given her hope that he was finally ready to settle down.

"What about Gisella? Does she know about this?"

Derrick stopped pacing, guilt flickered across his expression.

"Don't tell me he hasn't told her."

Derrick hedged. "Look, honey. There's a real good chance Charlie and Gisella may be breaking up."

"What? But Charlie's crazy about Gisella. They're supposed to be getting engaged." This didn't make sense.

Derrick started pacing again.

Isabella eyed her husband suspiciously. "Why would they break up?"

Derrick remained quiet.

"Who broke up with whom?" she needled.

"C'mon, honey. I don't butt into Charlie's business."

"Since when?" She climbed out of bed. "The Kappas huddle together at that barbershop every weekend and do nothing but gossip and high-five each other."

He tried to look insulted, but didn't quite pull it off.

"Charlie broke up with her and didn't tell her why, didn't he?" Isabella asked. "And something tells me the Kappas had something to do with it."

"That's not true," Derrick protested.

Isabella crossed her arms and tapped her foot.

"We just asked Charlie to evaluate his motivations for getting married. We thought it seemed like an awfully big coincidence his falling in love the same time he'd been given a death sentence."

"Oh, did you now, Dr. Phil?"

"C'mon, Bella. Don't be like that. What he was doing wasn't fair to Gisella. Surely you can see that."

"I'm calling Gisella." She rushed back to the bed and reached for the phone.

Derrick flew across the bedroom, dove over the bed and jabbed his hand against the receiver to hang up the line. "We promised Charlie we wouldn't tell her."

"*You're* not. I am," she said. "Gisella is *my* friend…and my business partner. I can't keep something like this from her. She deserves to know."

Derrick cocked his head. "It's not our place."

"It wasn't your place to tell Charlie to break up with Gisella, but that didn't stop you, now did it?" She watched another flicker of guilt cross his features. "I expected this kind of behavior from Taariq and Hylan. A party ain't party unless Charlie Masters is there, right? But you…"

"So what are you saying?" Derrick challenged. "You want her to fall in love with Charlie just so she can watch him die? Is that what you want her to do?"

"It should be her choice."

"No. It's *his* choice," he argued, his eyes glossed with tears. "It's Charlie's decision, and we *will* respect that." He watched her jaw harden and then added. "Please, Bella. For me."

Isabella's resolve held until she watched a tear streak down her husband's cheek. She cupped his face and pressed his head against her bosom. "All right…we'll do things your way."

"Thank you, baby."

Gisella promised herself that she wasn't going to cry.

For seven days, she kept that promise…until Sunday morning when she was soaking in her hot bubble bath with her green cucumber mask. One moment she was fine, and in the next she was a blubbering mess.

How could she have been so stubborn, hard-headed and foolish?

Breaking up with Robert had been hard, but the pain in her heart now was stronger than anything she'd ever experienced. Reviewing the past week, Gisella realized that she had been more or less a walking zombie. She opened the shop at the crack of dawn and didn't leave until the dead of night. She did everything she could to keep busy.

At night, she fought the temptation of even fantasizing

about Charlie, but lately, even that was getting harder and harder to do. She *did* want to see his face again, hear his voice. As her sobs bounced and echoed off the bathroom tile, she wondered how a man could make love the way he did and not feel anything.

Thereafter, every sentence started with *how* and *why,* and it continued until her head pounded mercilessly with a migraine.

"Gisella?"

At the sound of her sister's voice, Gisella made a lousy attempt to stem the flow of tears.

"Gisella, are you all right in there?"

She tried to respond, but all she could manage was more crying and sobbing.

The door flew open, and Anna rushed into the bathroom. Despite the water, bubbles and even the hardening cucumber mask, Gisella wrapped her arms around her big sister and cried until her heart was content.

"Shh. It's okay," Anna assured her. "Shh. It's going to be okay."

An hour later, Anna helped her sister out of the cold water, scrubbed her face and got her into bed. She instantly shifted into mother mode and fixed her something to eat and gave her aspirins for her headache.

She stayed with Gisella until she'd curled up in bed and fallen into a deep, exhausted sleep. This was exactly the heartbreak Anna had hoped her sister would avoid. But when Charlie Masters entered the picture, she and the Lonely Hearts knew that it was just a matter of time.

Still, there had been a sliver of hope that Charlie had

changed, but life just proved that you can't teach an old dog a new trick. Anna sat on the edge of her sister's bed and lovingly finger-combed a few strands of hair from her sleeping face. Seeing Gisella look so childlike and vulnerable tugged at her heartstrings and renewed her anger.

Anna returned to her sister's bathroom and picked up the wet towels and straightened up when her gaze snagged on something in the small wastebasket.

A pregnancy test.

A positive pregnancy test.

Charlie wasn't going to answer the phone. He lacked the strength or even the desire to talk to anyone. A second before the call transferred to voicemail, he shot an arm out from beneath the piles of sheets and comforters to grab the receiver.

"Y-yeah."

"Mr. Masters, this is Todd down at the front desk. You have a visitor down here."

Charlie groaned. "N-no. No visitors tonight, Todd."

"Yes, sir. But she's insisting that you'll want to talk to her."

"If it's your crazy sister Lexi—"

"No, sir. She says her name is Anna Jacobs."

Charlie sat straight up. "Anna?" He tried to defog his brain. "What is she doing here?"

"I don't know, sir. Should I ask her?"

He scrambled out of bed, trying to think. Was it Gisella? Had something happened?

"Sir?"

"Uh. Uh." He glanced at himself in pajamas and a

week-old beard. "Send her up." Charlie slammed the phone down and rushed to make himself presentable. All the while, his brain conjured up horrible scenarios of why Anna was there. Surely it was to deliver bad news. An illness? An accident?

When the doorbell rang, Charlie raced to the front door while still pulling a T-shirt over his head. When he finally jerked it open to his old college friend on the other side, he didn't greet her with the traditional "Hello" or "How are you?" But with a "Is she okay?"

Anna's eyebrows climbed. "I'd love to come in. Thank you." She stepped into his apartment. "It's good to see that you look like crap, too."

Charlie rolled his eyes, shut the door and waited with his heart clogging his throat. When she seemed content to inch her way through the apartment, pretending to be interested in the paintings and the knickknacks on the wall, his patience snapped. "Just spit it out. What's wrong with Gisella?"

Anna glanced over her shoulder and speared him with an icy glare. "Why do you care? Surely you've moved on to the next chick, right?"

Feeling the room tilt, Charlie closed his eyes and braced one hand against the wall. "Look, it's not what it looks like."

"Oh?" She crossed her arms. "And what does it look like *exactly?*"

Charlie sighed. Surely if something had happened to Gisella she would have said so by now. "That I'm…up to my old ways. That—that I was only after her for one thing."

"And you're suggesting that's *not* what happened?"

He shook his head, convinced she wouldn't believe

him. Instead of the expected yelling and cursing, Anna remained silent.

Charlie glanced up and was stunned by the tears streaming down her face.

"I wish I could believe you," she said. "But I have a sister at home crying her eyes out, and I know your reputation firsthand."

"Look, Anna. I don't expect you to believe me, but I love your sister."

"You have a funny way of showing it."

Tears now splashed down Charlie's face. "Trust me. I'm doing what's best for her."

"And will you do what's best for your *child* as well?"

Stunned, Charlie stared. "Gisella's…?"

"I think the word you're looking for is *pregnant*. The question is, are you man enough to do the right thing?"

A baby. His laughter started as a low rumble and grew into a loud raucous roar that vibrated off the walls.

Anna cocked her head, wondering about his sanity.

Charlie couldn't get over how cruel life could be. He made the mistake of removing his hand from the wall and when he took a step, he dropped like a stone.

"Charlie!" Anna rushed over to him.

He tried to laugh the incident off, but Anna wasn't buying. "What the hell is going on with you?" she asked. "And I want the truth."

Chapter 25

Gisella cried so much that she became used to the taste of her salty tears. By morning, she promised to pull herself back together. She was a strong woman, and somehow, someway, she would get through this. She just wished it didn't hurt so bad. She hugged the bed's pillow tighter while her heart continued to break.

"It's okay. Don't cry," Charlie's voice drifted over the shell of her ear.

No. No. She didn't want Fantasy Charlie there. If she couldn't have the real thing, she didn't want anything at all.

"It's okay, baby. I'm here."

A soft kiss was pressed against the back of her neck and caused a delicious tingle to ripple down her spine. She moaned, slowly allowing this fantasy to play out. Arms slid across her body and pulled her back to settle into a comfortable spoon position.

"I'm so sorry, baby." He kissed her again. "I'm so sorry I hurt you."

His hand now caressed her belly. "Can you ever forgive me?"

She desperately wanted to, but she couldn't get the words out.

"I thought I was doing what was best," he whispered. "I love you. I never stopped loving you. I swear there's no one else." He pulled her even closer. "I was so stupid."

It was probably the sound of his broken sobs that finally penetrated her foggy brain and forced her to open her eyes. This was no fantasy.

Gisella covered the hand over her belly and rolled over to face the man lying beside her. She was shocked at his haggard look, his scruffy beard and watery eyes. And yet, he was still able to steal her breath.

"Hey, you," he whispered.

Fresh tears blurred her vision while a whirlwind of emotions swirled inside of her. "What are you doing here?"

"I came to beg you for forgiveness…and to tell you the truth about why I pushed you away." With the pads of his thumbs, he wiped her face dry and started from the beginning.

By the time he was through, she was crying again. She hammered him with questions and mentally tried to rebel against his doctor's diagnosis. When she realized that she was acting just as he'd feared, she showered him with words of encouragement.

"Don't worry, sweetheart," she said. "We can get through this…together."

There was no doubt that she'd forgiven him. She was kissing and holding him so tight that he could scarcely breathe. But Charlie had no complaints, especially when she pulled her nightgown over her head and revealed the provocative curves he'd spent the last week trying to forget.

As always their bodies snapped together like the perfect puzzle. She lay back with her eyes sparkling while he stretched above her. He entered her with ease. Their mouths fed hungrily upon each other. Arms circling his neck, Gisella squeezed her inner muscles for each slow thrust of his hips.

"Oh, Gisella," he moaned, losing himself in her sweet body. Their rhythm picked up speed and the lovers grew wild with passion and their bodies soon became dewy with sweat.

Gisella was coming, surging over the edge and calling out Charlie's name.

They shuddered together in an orgasm that seemed to go on forever. She kissed his shoulders and he pressed his lips against her forehead.

"I still want to marry you," he whispered. "That's if you'll have me."

She hugged him tight and smiled up at him. "I'll marry you anytime, anywhere and anyplace."

Charlie quickly rolled over and retrieved the blue box from the pocket of his pants strewn on the floor. "I was supposed to give this to you last week."

Gisella popped open the box and gasped.

"This makes it official," Charlie said. He kissed her again and slid the ring onto her finger. "I love you."

"I love you, too." She hesitated. "There's something I have to tell you. I'm pregnant."

A new smile exploded across Charlie's face. He didn't want to ruin the moment by telling her that he already knew about the baby. Instead, he pulled her close and made love to her again.

And again.

And again.

"I don't understand," Charlie said. "Swing that back by me."

Dr. Weiner shifted awkwardly in his chair. He braided and unbraided his fingers several times before he repeated the results of Charlie's lab work. "I don't know how this mix-up happened, but I want you to know that I'm extremely sorry."

Charlie shook his head and prayed that his hearing hadn't failed him. "So, I *don't* have aplastic anemia?" he asked for the third time. "I'm not dying."

Embarrassed, the doctor shook his head. "The best we can figure is that there was some kind of screw-up at the lab. Your samples were switched with another patient's."

"Switched?"

"Oh, baby." Gisella grabbed Charlie's hand and squeezed. When Dr. Weiner had called them that morning, they had dropped everything and rushed right over. They agreed that they were in this together. No matter what the diagnosis, they would face it head on—and they would fight.

Fight for their love.

Fight for their future.

While happy tears filled Gisella's eyes, Charlie was busy connecting other dots. "Dr. Weiner, does Lexi Thomas still work here?"

Gisella's head swung toward the doctor. "She *works* here?"

Dr. Weiner blinked, clearly surprised by the question. "Nurse Thomas left the practice last month. Why?"

Charlie drew in an angry breath. "I don't believe this."

"You don't think she was crazy enough to deliberately switch your lab results?" Gisella asked.

"Of course she would. She vandalized my car, trashed and stole things out of my apartment. With her working here, how hard would it have been to switch my lab results?"

"Whoa. Whoa." Dr. Weiner held up his hands. "I don't know what you're talking about, but the accusations you're leveling are serious. Do you have proof of any of this?"

Charlie laughed. "Of course not. She's too clever for that." He clenched and unclenched his fist. He wished he could do more than issue a restraining order. At this point he was just glad that he didn't own a pet rabbit.

"What about his headaches and dizzy spells?" Gisella asked, patting Charlie's arms in hopes to calm him down. "If he doesn't have aplastic anemia something has to be wrong."

"There is." Dr. Weiner drew a deep breath. "All tests indicate that you have type 2 diabetes, and, of course, we've always known about your borderline high blood pressure. The dizziness and vertigo can occur when your blood sugar shoots up. It's definitely the culprit behind the migraines."

"That's it?" Charlie asked almost laughing. "Diabetes?"

"Diabetes is still a serious matter. The Centers for

Disease Control and Prevention considers diabetes to be a pandemic in America. The good news is now that we know what's wrong with you, we can work to control it."

"But it's not exactly the same as having a couple of months to live," Gisella cut in. Her relief so strong it caused her to laugh.

"No. With any luck Charlie will be with us for a long time." Dr. Weiner looked at Charlie. "Again. I want to express my sincere apology for this lab screw-up. I find it hard to believe that any member of my staff would have purposely switched lab results. I also want to point out that if you'd come in earlier for the additional testing then this wouldn't have carried out as long as it has."

At this moment, Charlie was too happy to be upset. "Can we have a few minutes alone?" he asked.

Weiner nodded. "Of course." He stood and left his office.

Immediately, Gisella launched into Charlie's arms and peppered his face with kisses. "Can you believe it, baby?"

He couldn't. After being so scared for seemingly so long, he felt as if he'd been given a second chance on life and in his arms was all he needed for happiness.

"You know what this means, don't you?" Gisella said. "I can't feed you any more of my chocolate."

Charlie laughed. "There's only one kind of chocolate I want from you, and I plan to have all I can eat every night."

Epilogue

One month later

Gisella and Charlie's hands overlapped as they gripped the knife and together sliced into a Sinful Chocolate popular creation—white chocolate and lemon cake. The happy couple smiled at the wedding photographer and then toward each other before shoving a handful of the decadent dessert into each other's faces.

Laughter rippled among the large gathering of friends and family and then a cheer went up when Charlie then tried to kiss and lick his wife's face clean. Armed with a new diet and medication, Charlie had learned to strike the perfect balance between having his cake and eating it, too.

"I love you, baby," he whispered, snapping their bodies together and dipping his head for a long soulful kiss. She tasted so sweet.

"Je t'aime aussi," she responded when he allowed her to come up for air.

Charlie groaned at the instant hard-on he acquired whenever Gisella spoke French. Now that they'd said their 'I do's, Charlie was ready to skip right to the honeymoon phase. So much so he found himself asking Gisella every five minutes, "Can we leave now?"

"Behave." She giggled and then allowed Anna to pull her away.

"I'm so happy for you, Gisella," Anna said, wrapping her arms around her baby sister. "I don't think the Lonely Hearts will admit it, but you've renewed our faith in love."

Gisella smiled and wiped away a stray tear from her sister's face. "I owe you so much. If you hadn't gone to see Charlie that night…"

Anna gave Gisella's waist a gentle squeeze. "I'm sure you would've done the same for me."

"In a heartbeat." She paused. "He's out there, you know. There's a perfect guy out there for you."

Anna shrugged. "Maybe. But until then, me and Sasha are going to be just fine."

Gisella smiled as her eyes snagged on Taariq as he walked across the lawn. *Maybe…*

Charlie laughed as his mother gripped his cheeks and tried to pinch the blood out of them. "My baby has made me so proud. Not only did you give me a beautiful daughter-in-law, but I'm finally getting my grandbaby."

"Anything for you, Mama." He kissed her cheek.

"Of course you know I was right," she added, releasing his cheeks. "Didn't I tell you if you found a woman who could cook like your mama then you had a winner?"

"That you did, Mama." He wrapped his arm around her.

"I just wish your father was here to see this day," she said. "Married and about to become a father. He would be so proud. I am."

"Thanks, Mom." He kissed her lovingly on her up-turned cheek.

"Mama Arlene," Taariq greeted her with a wide smile. "I don't know if Charlie told you, but we talked it over, and he's completely cool with calling me 'Daddy.' All you have to do now is accept my proposal. I'll make an honest woman out of you."

"You're so bad." Arlene blushed as she gave Taariq a welcoming hug. "Now when are *you* getting married?"

"As soon as you say yes."

She rolled her eyes. "You just love me for my fried chicken."

"That's not true. You make a mean potato pie, too."

Arlene laughed and then continued to giggle like a school-girl when Taariq asked for a dance. As he led her to the pavilion before the band, Charlie was left to shake his head.

"So you finally did it," Hylan said, slapping his large hand across Charlie's back. "You waved the white flag and surrendered to the enemy."

Charlie laughed and rolled his eyes. "Don't start that with me."

"What?" He hunched his shoulders. "I'm just saying. We were supposed to be playas for life. Remember?"

Derrick rushed up behind Hylan and quickly put him into a headlock. "Whatever he's saying, don't listen to him."

"Oh, he's harmless." Charlie chuckled. "I'm just waiting for the day when he starts waving his own white flag."

"It'll never happen," Hylan croaked from under Derrick's arm and tried to tap out.

"It doesn't make any sense to be so hard-headed," Derrick said, releasing him.

Hylan sucked in a deep breath and then playfully sent a left jab against Derrick's shoulder. "Mark my words. A brother like me ain't going down without a fight. You'll have to pry my playa's card out of my cold dead hands."

"All right," Derrick said. "We're going to hold you to that."

"Charlie, man," Stanley said, joining the group. "Your wife's cake is off the hook. What's her secret, man?"

"She didn't make this cake. Her assistant Pamela insisted on making the cake as a gift. She did a good job."

"Pamela, huh? Where is she?" Stanley turned to survey the crowd. "Maybe I'll marry her."

"I'm sure she'll be thrilled to hear it." Charlie laughed. "Start with baby steps. Try to get a date first."

"Or try to get a woman to stand still long enough for you introduce yourself."

"Ha. Ha. Y'all gonna get enough messing with me." Stanley scanned the crowd again. "There's gotta be someone here I can hook up with. Weddings are the best places for single people to hook up. That and funerals."

Hylan and Charlie just stared him.

"What? It's what I heard."

"We're going to pray for you," Hylan said.

"Whatever." Stanley moved closer to Charlie. "So now that you're off the market, what do you say to passing a playa like me your infamous little black book? I've heard that it's a pretty thick book."

"A playa like you?" Hylan snickered. "If anyone should inherit the Holy Grail from my man here, it should be me."

"Guys, guys. As much as I'd like to improve your whack game, I can't. Gisella and I had a nice farewell ceremony and then tossed the book into the fireplace."

Hylan and Stanley blinked and then both pointed at him accusingly. "Judas!"

Derrick and Charlie laughed.

"What do a couple of married women have to do to get a dance with their husbands?"

Derrick and Charlie turned toward their smiling wives.

"Not a thing," Charlie said, taking his wife into his arms. "Of course I'm looking forward to a little private dancing," he whispered as he led her toward the music.

"Oh, you'll get your dance, Mr. Masters. That and a whole lot more."

"That's what I'm counting on, Mrs. Masters. That's what I'm counting on."

REQUEST YOUR FREE BOOKS!

2 FREE NOVELS
PLUS 2 *FREE GIFTS!*

KIMANI™
ROMANCE

Love's ultimate destination!

**A mistake from the past
ignites a fiery future....**

NEW YORK TIMES BESTSELLING AUTHOR

BRENDA
JACKSON

FIRE AND DESIRE

A Madaris Family Novel

When Corinthians Avery snuck into a hotel room to seduce
Dex Madaris, it was Trevor Grant who emerged from the
shower to find her wearing next to nothing, and informed
her Dex was at home, happily married.

Two years later, traveling with Trevor on business,
Corinthians tries to avoid him, but his sexy smile sets her
on fire. And when a dangerous situation arises, they find
fear turning to feverish desire, never realizing that one
passionate night will change their lives forever....

*Available the first week of January 2009
wherever books are sold.*

ARABESQUE®

**www.kimanipress.com
www.myspace.com/kimanipress**

KPBJ0540109

New York Times Bestselling Author

BRENDA JACKSON

invites you to continue your journey
with the always sexy and always satisfying
Madaris family novels....

FIRE AND DESIRE
January 2009

SECRET LOVE
February 2009

TRUE LOVE
March 2009

SURRENDER
April 2009

ARABESQUE®

www.kimanipress.com
www.myspace.com/kimanipress